CAPTIVE

CAPTIVE

A. J. GRAINGER

SIMON & SCHUSTER BFYR

NEW YORK   LONDON   TORONTO   SYDNEY   NEW DELHI

SIMON & SCHUSTER BFYR

An imprint of Simon & Schuster Children's Publishing Division
1230 Avenue of the Americas, New York, New York 10020

First published in Great Britain in 2015 by Simon & Schuster UK, Ltd.
First US edition 2015

For information about special discounts for bulk purchases, please contact Simon & Schuster Special Sales at 1-866-506-1949 or business@simonandschuster.com.
The Simon & Schuster Speakers Bureau can bring authors to your live event. For more information or to book an event, contact the Simon & Schuster Speakers Bureau at 1-866-248-3049 or visit our website at www.simonspeakers.com.
Jacket design by Krista Vossen
Interior design by Hilary Zarycky
The text for this book is set in Electra LT Std.
Manufactured in the United States of America
2 4 6 8 10 9 7 5 3 1
Library of Congress Cataloging-in-Publication Data
Grainger, A. J. (Annalie J.)
Captive / A.J. Grainger. — 1st edition.
pages cm
Summary: Sixteen-year-old Robyn Knollys-Green struggles to keep faith in her father, the British Prime Minister, while being held hostage by a group of extremist activists that includes an attractive, kind young man called Talon.
ISBN 978-1-4814-2903-0 (hardcover)
ISBN 978-1-4814-2905-4 (eBook)
[1. Hostages—Fiction. 2. Kidnapping—Fiction. 3. Terrorism—Fiction. 4. Children of politicians—Fiction. 5. Fathers and daughters—Fiction. 6. Pharmaceutical industry—Fiction. 7. England—Fiction.] I. Title.
PZ7.1.G72Cap 2015
[Fic]—dc23
2014033632

For Adam

Acknowledgments

A lot of tea, biscuits, angst, and far too many tears went into writing *Captive* and I couldn't have done it without the following people:

My UK agent, Jane Finigan, and everyone else at Lutyens and Rubinstein.

My US agent, David Forrer at InkWell Management.

My wonderful editors, Elv Moody and Christian Trimmer. This book is so much better because of them. A huge thank-you also to their brilliant assistants, Rachel Mann and Catherine Laudone, as well as everyone else at S&S for their hard work and belief in me and this book.

My friends, most particularly Natto, Ellie, Fran, Chezzie, Lucie, Tim, and Yusur.

My family, especially my parents (all four of them).

And lastly my husband. Adam, this book is dedicated to you because—like so many of the wonderful things in my life—it wouldn't exist without you.

CAPTIVE

January

Paris. The coldest winter in thirty years. The shivering limbs of trees pierce the deadened sky in the Jardin du Luxembourg. Ice clings to the abdomen of the Eiffel Tower. My father's blood is a vivid stain on the white-laced pavement outside the hotel. In the distance, the sirens scream, but they are too far away.

Dad is already losing consciousness, his eyes rolling back to milky white, his mouth drooping as the bright-red blood spills out across the bright-white snow. All around me people are shouting. Nearby, one of Dad's bodyguards is yelling into a radio, "Request urgent backup. The prime minister has been shot. Repeat: The prime minister has been shot."

And someone is screaming.

It is a long time before I realize it is me.

Three months later

CHAPTER ONE

My three-year-old sister, Addy, is playing with her Baby Betty doll on the stairs of Number 10. Her collection of dolls is pushed up against the wooden paneling of the fourteenth step, the one that takes the stairs around the first bend. She shouldn't be here. She should be up in our flat, getting ready to leave. She is so intent on her game that for a while she doesn't notice me sit down behind her. When she does look up, her face becomes one big, open smile.

"Byn, cuddle," she says, sitting down in my lap.

"Why aren't you dressed yet?" I ask, blowing a raspberry on her baby potbelly. She squeals, slapping me around the head. I let her go and she slides off my lap, taking her doll with her, its head bumping on the step as she reaches for another of her toys: a fluffy giraffe that the Kenyan president's wife gave her on a state visit last year. A wisp of white-blond hair twists like a curly tail on the nape of my sister's neck. I tug it gently, watching it straighten and curl, straighten and curl as a voice rises from the hallway below. I shift Addy so I can peer through the banister.

"Thanks for seeing me at such short notice, Stephen. I appreciate it," a tall man with round wire-framed glasses is saying. It's Michael Bell, the head of Bell-Barkov and one of Dad's oldest friends. He is ridiculously dressed as usual, a canary-yellow tie matched with a pale-pink shirt. If looking like a boiled sweet were in this season, Michael would be right on trend.

"Hello, Robyn," Michael says, looking up and cutting off my train of thought. Addy appears next to me, waving her doll at him through the banister. "How are you, girls?" he asks. "Annabelle was asking after you—"

Dad cuts him short. "I'm due at Westminster shortly, and I've got back-to-backs all day. I can only give you five minutes, tops."

Michael gives a brief wave, and then the two of them disappear from view down one of the corridors.

Shadow, my cat, brushes my arm. He is creeping up the stairs, his eyes on Addy. Addy's love for Shadow is unconditional and frequently painful, for the cat. She looks up at the wrong moment (for Shadow) and launches herself at him. With a cry of "Hug Kitty," she squeezes him tight, and the inevitable happens. Shadow lashes out and catches Addy on her cheek. It is a minuscule scratch, but baby howls join cat yowls. Thankfully, Dad and Michael have passed through the interconnecting door into Number 11, so they won't be disturbed.

I scoop Addy up with one hand and pat Shadow soothingly with the other.

"Kitty scratch! Bad kitty." She thumps Shadow on the back.

"Hey, hey," I say, acting as peace ambassador. "Shadow was scared. He didn't mean to scratch you. You have to be gentle, Ads. Remember, like I showed you." I scoot back to sit against the wall, with Addy curled in on one side and Shadow on the other. Shadow lets out a resentful purr as I tickle him under the ears. His second purr is calmer as the hair on his haunches settles down.

Addy sniffs again. "Stroke Kitty?" she asks, wiping her eyes.

"Stroke him gently. That's it." Addy runs her hand along Shadow's back, the wrong way, and her tap on his head has more in common with a punch. Shadow looks at me as if to say, *Yeah right,* and makes a break for it. Addy's mouth opens again, but before she can form a yell, Mum calls my name from farther down the corridor. She comes out of one of the offices on this floor, dressed in a neat blue knee-length dress and matching two-inch heels. She looks like she's going to a wedding or a fashion shoot. When the nation's press camp out on your front door with their long-angle camera lenses, even the school run can feel like the runway at Paris Fashion Week. Ever since a hideous moment last year, at the prince's christening at Westminster Abbey, when Mum wore a pleated skirt on a windy day and the entire country saw her Spanx, she's worn tunic dresses, in heavy material, to the knee, which even a tornado couldn't blow skyward.

Mum keeps out of Dad's work as much as possible. In politics, her motto is "See no evil, hear no evil." She thinks you can't be responsible for what you don't know. She's wrong. Dad says the only way to thrive here, in these cramped and fusty old rooms, full of too many files, boxes, aides, press assistants, and researchers, is to either know everything, or to appear to. Ultimately it is not what you know, or even who you know—it's what people say you know that is important. People think my dad knows everything. Other people's secrets are his currency.

"Adriana isn't even dressed, Robyn," Mum says, as if I'm the nanny. "Where is Karen?" (The actual nanny.) "Come here, Addy, darling."

I carry my sister up to Mum. Addy cries out for her toys, her legs kicking out. One catches the picture of an ex-prime minister hanging at the top of the stairs, nearly knocking it to the floor. Mum lunges for Addy, and I lunge for the photo. Addy settles as soon as she's in Mum's arms, clamping herself to Mum's body like a baby koala. Mum scoots her onto one hip. "Are you packed? I'd like you to show me which schoolbooks you are planning on bringing with you, Robyn. It'll be very quiet in Cheshire, and you can make a start on some of the reading you have to do for next term."

Addy is curved into Mum's body, head on one side,

peering up at me. I make a funny face at her and she does her shy thing, pulling Mum's long brown hair over her face.

"Are you listening to me?" Mum asks.

"Yes. Schoolbooks. Quiet. Start reading."

Mum's face registers hurt, and I feel bad and grumpy in equal measure. "I'll do some work, but I'm taking my camera as well."

"If you must—but schoolwork first. I know these last few months have been hard, but you can't afford to let your grades slip. You've got exams coming up."

I tickle Addy under the chin, making her squeal, and then change the subject. "Will Dad be all right without us?"

"I expect so. It's only for four days." Mum's lips pinch, the way they always do when someone brings up Dad. "Although heaven knows when he'll ever remember to take his pills. I'll speak to one of the Garden Room Girls about reminding him." The Garden Room Girls are the bank of secretaries who work here round the clock, so called because they are based in the room off the garden. Super unoriginal and super sexist. It's a holdover from years ago. They're not even all women these days.

"He'll never get full use of his shoulder back, will he?" I say.

"I think it's safe to say he won't be playing tennis again anytime soon. Mind you, after that humiliating performance against the US president at Chequers last year, it's probably no bad thing." She stops as she sees my eyes mist with tears that have nothing to do with Dad losing 6–2 to the US president and then hurling his tennis racket at the net. "Oh, Robyn, sweetheart." She tucks a strand of my hair behind my ear before I can duck out of reach. "We're safe. No one will hurt you or your father again."

People think the British prime minister must live in some really palatial pad, with state-of-the-art everything, but our flat here is actually much smaller than our real home in West Kensington, and the whole thing would probably fit in the ballroom at Groundings, Granny and Grandpa's estate in Cheshire. Mum says the PM's flat is dusty and dirty and needs a "jolly good refit," and she hates not having all our furniture here. Most of it had to go into storage when Dad became PM four years ago. Mum says she can't remember what half of it looks like now. To which Dad always replies, "How can you miss it, then?"

The garden here is nice, though—an L-shaped stretch of grass and trees. I planted a rose tree when we first moved in. It was from a cutting of one of Granny's trees. "A little piece of the countryside in that smelly city," she said. I used to love going out to the garden, even in winter, but since the shooting in January, it seems too exposed. The walls don't seem high enough, and the windows of Numbers 10, 11, and 12 stare down like lidless eyes on three of its sides. Anyone could be hiding inside them with a gun. Logic and the security services tell me that nothing like that will ever happen again. The man responsible for the shooting has been arrested, and security has been stepped up like crazy over the past three months. Four more police officers at the gates, two extra armed guards patrol the walls, and loads more plainclothes detectives in the surrounding areas, keeping an eye on things. But sometimes your brain doesn't want to listen to logic. It just wants to have a little freak-out anyway.

I turn away from the window in my room. There's a mass of stuff on my bed waiting to be packed. T-shirts, jeans, sweaters, thick socks, and rain boots. It's cold at Granny and Grandpa's, even in spring. On top of the pile of clothes is the digital SLR camera I got for Christmas. I don't really know why I got into photography. Actually, I do. His name is Ed Taylor. He's in the year above me, and he taught me how to use a camera during lunch breaks last year. He taught me a couple of other things too, like the fact that just because you have gorgeous floppy hair, are artistic, and know the exact settings on a digital camera to capture the perfect cityscape at night doesn't mean you aren't also a massive jerk. Our fledgling relationship ended when I caught him kissing Cassandra Fulgate at a Christmas party.

Still, he taught me a bit about photography, so not all bad.

Addy's princess doll is lying on the floor by my bed. I pick her up and put her on the table, bending her legs so she can sit on the edge. She smiles her smug smile at me. This is the kind of daughter the PM should have—a plastic one with neat blond hair and a designer outfit for every occasion. The public thinks they know me because some fashion magazine is able to determine that I buy my clothes from Topshop rather than Prada, and because some person we met once for a few minutes on a crowded beach in Morocco two years ago wrote a piece for the Femail about "The Real Knollys-Greens." They called me the "shy and thoughtful elder daughter" with a "stubborn streak." "She knows her own mind," the author wrote, "and she doesn't always agree with her father's policies." I reckon the latter was because I was reading *Animal Farm*. It was for a school project, but the journalist wouldn't know that from the very short conversation she had with me.

I take the shutter off my camera and snap a few shots of the doll, zooming in really tight to her face. There's a potted plant on my dressing table, and I position it in front of the doll, poking my camera through the leaves to take a couple of "pap shots." When I first started taking pictures, it amused me to photograph the paparazzi who were snapping photos of us. They did not like it. After one photographer got particularly nasty, Dad suggested I stick to taking photos of inanimate objects like trees and flowers. He said they tend to be "less sensitive."

The door to my bedroom opens and Dad comes in, a tie in each hand, a magazine tucked under one arm. He looks tired, but then he always does these days, especially after meetings with Michael. "Ah, here you are," he says. "I need your advice. Red or yellow?"

The red, a near crimson, against his white shirt, is too much like blood on snow. "Yellow," I say quickly.

"Jolly good." He drops the red tie and the magazine on my desk chair so he can wrap the yellow one around his neck. His jaw sets in pain as he rotates his shoulder. I wince, and Dad immediately smiles reassuringly. "Just a twinge."

"Did you take your painkillers this morning?"

"Yes, Nurse Robyn." He pushes the end of the tie through its knot. "Straight?"

I nod, glancing down at the magazine. *Science Today.* One of the headlines reads BELL-BARKOV'S LANDMARK KIDNEY DRUG AMABIM-F GIVEN INTERNATIONAL GO-AHEAD.

"Did Michael bring you that?"

"Oh. Yes." He can see I'm lining up for another question, so he quickly changes the subject. "Are you nearly ready to go? Your mum wants to be there by lunchtime. Gordon informed me that two armed police officers on motorcycles will escort you."

My heart thumps in my throat. I am worried about traveling down to Cheshire. It'll be the longest trip I've taken since we came back from Paris.

Dad reads my expression. "You'll be fine, Robyn. You need to be brave, my darling."

I wish everyone would stop telling me that everything is going to be okay and that I need to trust the security services. The truth is, I'm scared. I can't stop thinking about what happened in Paris. Dad nearly died that day. *I* nearly died that day. The world is not safe. I know that now and I can't *un*know it, however much people might tell me to. "You'll take the car to Whitehall again today, won't you?" I ask. Before the assassination attempt, Dad used to walk to Parliament. I dread the thought of anything happening to him again. He doesn't look after himself the way he should. He's too busy thinking about other things, like running the country.

"Of course. 'Keep buggering on,'" he says, quoting Winston Churchill. He always quotes other people when he wants to avoid talking about something. Familiar worry lines spring up on his face, and I know I'm right. He's concerned too, but he'll never admit it. There's anxiety in his eyes. They are the exact same shade and color as mine. Everything else about me is my mum's: long dark hair; pointy chin and freckles; lopsided nose. But my eyes are my dad's. "Chameleon eyes," Mum calls them—sometimes green, sometimes brown, and sometimes almost golden. They change with the seasons, and our moods.

"Have you said good-bye to Poppy?" Dad asks, smiling more broadly than the question warrants.

"No," I snap, irritated that Dad is pretending everything is okay, just like everyone else is. Then I instantly adjust my tone. Dad has enough worries. He doesn't need me adding to them. "I'm going to see her now."

"Well, best get a move on. You'll be leaving in twenty minutes."

Number 10 and Number 11, where the chancellor of the exchequer lives with his wife and daughter, Poppy, are joined by interconnecting doors. Poppy is nearly seventeen like me. We didn't know each other very well before we both moved here four years ago, but we've gotten really close since then. She is the only one who gets what it is like to live in this place, protected, guarded, and constantly watched. It's odd to be so important and yet so utterly ignored. My safety is everyone's priority, but no one is really interested in me. Unless I do something wrong, of course. Then a lot of people are very interested.

Poppy is reading a book on her bed when I come into her room, her legs propped up. (Someone told her this would prevent varicose veins. I told her she didn't need to worry about that for at least another fifty years, but Poppy said she didn't care. Her legs are her best feature, and she intends to keep them that way.) She puts the book down as soon as she sees me.

I take my camera out of my shoulder bag, and Poppy immediately shrieks and covers her face. "Don't take any photos of me! You always give me a big nose." She fingers her perfect little button nose.

"It's a camera, Poppy. It just records what it sees."

"No. It's the angles you use. All odd and distorted."

"Is that the technical term?"

"Shut up. You know what I mean."

I sit next to her on the bed.

"Are you going to be back for Millie's party on Saturday?" she asks.

"Probably not. Mum wants to come back late Sunday evening."

"Ed might be there."

"Yeah, and so will Cassandra."

"She's a cow, isn't she? I mean, she knew you two were . . . Wait, what were you two doing? I mean, aside from taking pretentious arty photos."

"Art is my life, Poppy. There is nothing for me beyond that."

She laughs as I meant her to. "You could get the train back. I'm sure Mum would pick you up from the station. Unless you don't want to go?"

"I hate those parties. There will be people we don't know there."

"Ooh, scary."

"And they always stare at me, or think it's hysterical to give me double shots so the PM's daughter ends up more hammered than anyone else."

"I'll be there. I promise to guard your drink and not let anyone else touch it."

"I just don't fancy it. Besides, Dad's really fussy about where I go now." That's not true. Dad wants me to move on and stop worrying. It's me who doesn't want to go out so much.

As usual, Poppy reads me so well. "You can't hide forever," she says.

I lift the camera to my face and take a snap of the corner of her room, where the shadow of the curtains creeps across the floor like a huge hand. I switch to black and white. If I get the shot right, the picture should look like a still straight out of a Hitchcock movie. "Watch me."

"I'm the chancellor's daughter, and you don't hear me complaining."

"Only because no one actually knows what the chancellor does, including half the cabinet. Dad's always saying, 'What does that chap next door do again?'"

"Oh, funny!"

I take the picture and then let the camera fall back into my lap. "I hate it here, Poppy."

"Only one more year to go."

"And then five more, when he runs again."

"He might not."

"Can you imagine my dad doing anything else?"

"He must have. He's only been PM four years."

"And he spent the eighteen years before that preparing to be PM. Let's face it, I'm stuck here." I glance across the Downing Street garden and over its high walls at Horse

Guards Parade. The early-bird tourists are already lining up for the first changing of the guard. A shadow moves at the corner of my eye, and I jump, but it's just Poppy.

"He's locked up," she says gently. "He can't come after your father again."

"But if not him, then someone else—"

There's a knock on the door, and Poppy's mum sticks her head around it to tell me that the car is here.

"Have fun in Cheshire and stop worrying about everything. It's all going to be fine," Poppy says. "And come back for the party on Saturday night. You're in danger of becoming a total loser."

I give one last nervous look out across the grounds and into the world beyond, then force a smile. "I'll try. And Poppy," I say at the door, "say cheese!" I snap a picture and dash down the corridor to the sound of her yelling, "I hate you, Robyn Knollys-Green! You better not post that online anywhere! I haven't got mascara on."

Ben is the police officer on duty out front today. He steps aside to let me out of the front door. "All ready for the trip, miss?" he asks. The door opens again before I can answer, and Addy dashes out, barreling into my legs. I catch her around the waist and swing her upward. Mum and Dad are right behind her. "You'll take your pills, won't you?" Mum is saying. "Every day, Stephen."

"How is it, Eliza, that you trust me to run the country but not my own life?"

"You care about the country," Mum says.

Dad turns to Ben. "Do you hear this? I bet you don't get this at home."

Ben smiles politely, but Mum's jaw tightens as she grits her teeth. "So I suppose you'll survive without us for a few days?" she says.

"'Liberty is one of the most precious gifts that Heaven has bestowed on mankind.'" Dad grins. "But I shall miss you, my love."

Mum steps back from his kiss, screwing her face up. "Stephen, darling, I've just done my lipstick."

Dad kisses Addy instead, taking her out of my arms and lifting her above his head, making her giggle. After giving her to Mum, who makes a big fuss of smoothing out the imaginary wrinkles in her dress, he turns to me. "You're a bit big to fling in the air. Be safe," he whispers, hugging me. It's brief, but for a sudden I'm caught up in the familiar smell of his aftershave and I'm protected, in a world where the shooting never happened. When he steps back, the April breeze whips up my spine. Dad and I haven't spoken much about what happened in Paris. Mum says this is unhealthy, but she wasn't there. Remembering is bad enough. I don't want to give words to the memories as well.

"Look after my family," Dad says to John, the special-ops

driver, who nods and replies, "Like they were my own." I want to make Dad promise me again that he will take a car to Parliament, but there's no time, and I know he won't want me making a fuss with all these people around.

Addy is whimpering by the time I get in the car, straining against her seat belt and kicking her little legs up and down. She's going to be restless the whole way to Cheshire. Dad pats the car door like it's a horse's flank. "Send my love to Granny and Grandpa. Bye, my darlings," he yells as we drive toward the gate. I turn to wave, but he's moved back to stand on the step and all I can see is his headless torso.

CHAPTER TWO

A man is standing on an upturned crate outside the mini supermarket by the Westminster tube station. His arms are spread wide, his head angled toward heaven. His mouth opens and closes with inaudible sounds, while behind him a poster flaps in the strong breeze. BE VIGILANT. REPORT ANY SUSPICIOUS BEHAVIOR. He is one of the religious nuts, the ones who believe that the global financial catastrophe five years ago was an act of God. We were being punished for worshipping the false idol Money.

The car takes a right at Parliament, passing Westminster Abbey, and drives along the north bank of the River Thames. I gaze back across at the murky brown water and Westminster Bridge. It would make a good photo: the bare black trees stenciled on the dead gray sky, the bridge disappearing behind the fog, the water punctuated by the light splattering of icy rain. If only my camera weren't in my bag in the boot of the car. I make a square with my fingers and hold it up to the window. *Click. Click.* Shift the angle as the road curves with the river. *Click*. I'll have to remember this view for when we drive back.

Addy, Mum, and I are spending the rest of the Easter vacation at Groundings. I overheard Mum saying to Dad that she thought a break from London would be good. She didn't say whether she meant it would be good for me or for her. She and Dad haven't exactly been getting along recently, or ever really.

Addy is sleeping now, murmuring to herself as she always does. I stare out of the window at the sky, which is as blank as a dead computer screen.

Mum flicks on the radio: ". . . a judge this morning refused to grant bail for Kyle 'Marble' Jefferies, the man accused of the attempted assassination—"

Mum switches the channel.

"Leave it," I say. "Please."

"Robyn, you know all of this," she says gently, but she turns the radio back to the BBC. I worry more when they try to keep things from me.

". . . shots were fired at the PM and his elder daughter as they were fleeing a hotel in Paris in January of this year, following a bomb threat. A small radical anticapitalist and animal rights group, Action for Change (the AFC), of which Jefferies is a member, claimed responsibility for the attack. Jefferies maintains that he worked alone, but experts believe it likely that a number of people were involved.

"The PM is believed to have been targeted because of his long-standing friendship with Michael Bell, the head of the UK's largest pharmaceutical company, Bell-Barkov. The pharma has come under attack from these extremists before, with Bell and his staff receiving death threats over their use of animals in laboratories and drug-testing practices.

"It is now believed that Jefferies was also behind the fire at Bell-Barkov's headquarters last October, although he denies the charges. The AFC has not claimed any involvement in the arson attack, which destroyed the company's research center and injured three security guards."

The day my father was shot was the most terrifying of my life. I hate Kyle Jefferies. I hope he never leaves prison. He's the reason I feel scared and worried all the time.

The news presenter has moved on to saying that Bell-Barkov is a major financial supporter of this government when Mum clicks the radio off. Silences fills the car until Addy cries out. She's awake and has dropped her toy lamb. Mum and I both jump, then Mum laughs. "We're all so twitchy." She reaches down in the seat well behind her to retrieve Lamby. Addy catches the lamb and kisses him over and over again with a loud *mwah, mwah* noise. Mum pats my knee, her eyes looking for reassurance in mine. I nod quickly, because my parents need to believe that I'm all right, but inside, my heart is thumping loudly. *Durdum durdum durdum durdum.*

"So," Mum says, a forced cheerfulness in her tone, "how

about a song? John . . . you're always good at this. What'll it be? 'Baa, Baa, Black Sheep'?"

"Well," John says, "personally I've always thought you couldn't beat the classic 'Twinkle, Twinkle, Little Star.'"

"'Twinkle, Twinkle' it is. Come on, Addy. This is one of your favorites." Mum flings her arms upward as her voice rises dangerously high. She is so desperate for everything to be okay. "It's such a gorgeous day, and it's so wonderful to be away from that bloody city."

I'm typing a text to Poppy (IN CAR WITH MUM. SHE'S SING-ING. HELP!) when John suddenly slams on the brakes. A car is parked diagonally across the road. My heart thuds its uneven beat. A sixth sense tells me that something isn't right. The car's bonnet sparkles in the sun, its metal flashing through the trees that grow thick and heavy along this stretch of road. The two motorcycles flanking us drive ahead to investigate, while John waits.

"John?" Mum asks, a hint of anxiety in her voice.

"It's all right, Mrs. Knollys-Green. Probably just a broken-down vehicle. We'll be on our way again any minute—"

He is cut off as the car in front of us explodes in vicious heat and searing light. The road beyond it disappears, and trees, dirt, and tarmac are flung upward in a *whoomph*. The once-blue sky on the horizon is obliterated by a swirling mass of smoke that's thrown over everything like a sudden darkness. The surrounding color shines brighter. The greenest green of the trees lining the road, the stark blackness of a bird's wing as the creature soars into the air, terrified by the noise. I imagine I can see a tear in the world: the point on this side of the car, where we are alive and safe, and the point beyond where the nightmare begins, and then even that is gone, swallowed up by crackling flames.

Mum turns around in her seat, tugging at her seat belt so she can rest her hand against Addy's knee. Tears are pouring down Addy's face. Mum's mouth moves, but I can't hear the words. There's something wrong with my ears, like someone turned on a tap in my head, and all I can hear is gushing water. My phone has slipped out of my hand and is lying in the footwell. I vaguely think about picking it up, but my body won't cooperate.

John is speaking, and I read his lips. "Just . . . fine." He smiles, his face opening up like a flower, and Addy seems to calm down.

They are all looking at me, and I am nodding as if I am fine too. Can't they hear the water? I tilt my head to try to dislodge the sound. The trees by the side of the road somersault, and bile rises in my throat. I level my head again and peer through the dark smog engulfing our car. The two motorcycle escorts have been flung from their bikes. One has pulled himself to standing and is limping as he drags his leg out from under the bike, but otherwise he looks okay.

The other man is lying motionless, his body crumpled at an awkward angle and his head concealed by the rising banks of the ditch at the side of the road. John is talking into his radio. Somewhere on the other end, a team of experts are planning our next move, calling in the army and trying to calculate the safest option while we wait for them. We have two options: stay here where we are sitting ducks, or risk running into an ambush by going back the way we've come.

A tree full of frightened birds soars up through the dirty air beside the car. I wonder what new noise has disturbed them. I still can't hear anything above the rushing in my ears. But John suddenly throws the car's gear stick into reverse. At the same moment my ears come unstuck. The water gurgles and disappears. Noise fills my eardrums again. Addy is screaming, and somewhere off in the woods, there is the sound of gunfire.

My neck snaps back as John executes a 180-degree turn at what feels like ninety miles an hour. Addy continues to yell. "It's okay, darling. It's okay," Mum says, but Addy probably can't hear her over the sound of her own wailing.

Trees, hedgerows, and ditches blur past us as the car eats up the road. My seat belt holds me fast. I tug on it sharply, only succeeding in pulling the bonds more securely around me. Addy is almost choking with sobs now, and her eyes are wide and terrified. Mum is trying to turn around, but the movement of the car keeps slamming her against the leather seat while my belt is still trying to suffocate me. Screw it. With a click, I release the lock and slide over to my sister, wrapping my arms around her trembling body. She wiggles into me, her little hand knotting in my T-shirt, but her cries ease. Although I realize that taking my belt off may not have been the smartest idea as the car hits another bump in the road and my head bashes into the roof.

"Robyn!" Mum shouts. "Put your belt on."

John takes the corner sharply, and I am flung forward. Mum cries out again. With an effort, I launch myself toward my seat, while still trying to keep hold of Addy's hand. But the car is moving too fast, and I need both my hands to stop myself from flying into the front seat. I end up sliding down into the well behind John. As I pull myself up again and fasten my seat belt, I catch a glimpse out the back window of a white van trailing us.

I don't have time to think anything of it, because the next bend in the road is acute and John misses it. The tires slide as he turns the steering wheel sharply to try and regain control. It's not enough. The car bounces, hits a crease in the road, and sky becomes earth becomes sky becomes earth as we spin over and over.

My head bangs against the window, and as I'm jolted away again, I lay my arm flat against Addy's chest. The car flips once more, and slams into a tree. Mum screams once and then everything is silent.

. . .

I am aware of sound—the thin, rhythmic drops of water from leaves, the rustling of a bird's feathers in the undergrowth, the whoosh of steam rising from the crushed bonnet of the car, the thick, wet glug of petrol thudding on tarmac. I open my eyes. The car is not upside down as I'd thought, and the world is the right way up. "Byn," whispers a voice that is barely a voice. Addy is staring at me from the prison of her car seat. "Byn?" she says again, her face its own question.

I muster up a smile. "Hey, munchkin."

There's a soft gurgle from the front passenger seat. "Mum?" The gurgle gets louder. I stretch forward as far as my still-fastened seat belt will allow. The back of the driver's seat is sticky. I know that if I look down at my knees, they will be red with blood, so I don't look. It's not mine.

"Mum?" I unfasten my seat belt and peer around at her. Her face is a white smudge against the leather seat, but she smiles weakly. "Is John . . . ?" I ask. I can't look.

"No . . . I think he's breathing. Just."

"I'm going to get help."

Mum shakes her head.

"I'm fine. I can get out. I'll stand farther up the road. Make sure they know where to find us. It's going to be all right." I reach down into the footwell and fumble around to retrieve my phone.

I'm sure my head has swelled to twice its normal size,

but otherwise I mostly feel fine. I try to open the door, but it won't move. I push harder and harder, until it gives suddenly and I fall out, hands and knees smacking the ground. A shadow falls over me. I look up and scream. A man—the figure is too big for a woman—is standing above me. Some sort of black ski mask covers his entire face except for his eyes and mouth. He tugs me upright. I let myself get my balance and then swivel sharply, right and left, because a moving target is harder to hold on to. I'm remembering my self-defense training, but it's more than that, like some sort of instinct that I didn't know I had is kicking in. He still has a firm grip on my arm.

"BACK OFF!" I scream right into his face, and at the same time I slam my knee between his legs. I hear a groan, and he finally lets go.

Then I begin to run, trying to put enough distance between us while fumbling to call for help on my phone. The man is on me again too quickly, though. He swipes the phone from my hand, and it lands with a loud crack on the pavement. I have no time to dodge his next attack, and he clamps me to his chest with arms as broad and solid as an oak door. The stench of sweat fills my nostrils. It is not fresh. This is sweat that has been sweated and dried, sweated and dried again with no thought of a shower. At least a few days' worth. I think of the various products in Mum's cabinet, like soldiers waiting for action, and try to conjure up the smell of chamomile bath salts, lemon talcum powder, lavender hand soap.

It doesn't work. I draw a deep breath. Sweat. Days-old sweat.

I wriggle and squirm, but it does no good.

"Calm down, Princess. We just want to talk, some-where more private, like." He nods his head in the direction of the white van, parked up on the other side of the road. Something sharp presses into the base of my spine, piercing my thin T-shirt. "Now move or I'll cut you. Scream and I'll cut you." Another prick of the blade.

He walks me down the road, and I remember something that Gordon, Dad's head of security, once said. He was talking about the time he'd spent in Colombia, where the threat of kidnapping is high. *You have a sixty-five percent chance of get-ting away in the first five minutes of being taken. Once you are in a vehicle, your chance of escape drops to thirty-five percent. Kick, scream, bite. Use the weapons you have. Do not let them get you into a vehicle.*

John has radioed for help. The entire British army should be on its way any second. I just have to hold out a little longer.

I kick.

I scream.

I bite.

His grip loosens. It's enough. I jam my elbow hard into the space between his ribs. He lets out an *oomph*, and I surge forward. He snatches for me, not managing to get ahold of me, but it's enough to knock me off balance. A pair of arms comes out of nowhere and catches me before my face can connect with the cold, hard pavement. I'm pinned to the ground, and someone leans over me. Someone new, someone who seems to have come out of nowhere. I can see his eyes through his mask. They are bright green, like light hitting deep water. His mouth moves through a word that I can barely believe is "Sorry" as he lifts a strong-smelling cloth to my face. The harsh chemical is a whoosh in my lungs; black moths cloud my vision, and consciousness recedes into darkness.

Addy is cranky. She's lying on the sofa at our flat in Downing Street, covered in chicken pox. Mum is beside her, holding both of her hands in an attempt to stop her scratching.

"We're not going, are we?" I say, leaning against the door frame.

Mum's eyes are dark pips in a white face. "Oh, darling. I'm sorry. I just can't leave her like this. We'll go later in the year. It has been a terrible January there anyway. They've had snow like you wouldn't believe. Maybe during summer recess . . . We could try again then. If your father ever takes any time off, we could maybe go—" Addy whimpers, trying to tug her hands from Mum's. "You mustn't scratch, darling," Mum says gently. Addy pulls harder, letting out a thin whine, her rosebud mouth puckering into a sulk. "Shh." Mum peels a sticky, featherlike strand of hair off my sister's forehead.

I push myself off the door frame and head down the

corridor. "Don't be too disappointed, sweetheart," Mum calls after me.

I wave vaguely over my shoulder.

The kitchen is dark, the winter sun barely piercing the cloud cover. I don't bother turning on the light. Instead I flick on the TV. Its screen casts a sallow glow over the room. Outside, the sky is gray. It's snowing in Paris. Poppy and I checked the weather report this morning. I was trying to get her to look at these amazing photos that Henri Cartier-Bresson took of the city, but she was totally disinterested. She mainly wanted to know if I was taking my new T-shirt to Paris and if I wasn't, could she borrow it. I refused to answer her question until she looked at three of the photos. There is one in particular, taken in black and white from one of the viewing platforms on the Eiffel Tower, that looks like a spider or some other huge insect is crawling up the side of the building. It is incredible, but Poppy just asked why it wasn't in color. I called her an ignoramus and said I was reconsidering our friendship. She stuck her tongue out at me.

"Are you ready to go?" Dad asks. He's standing in the doorway to the kitchen.

"We're not going."

"Says who?"

"Mum, because Addy—"

"Is sick, yes, but you're not. So, my darling daughter, how do you fancy three days in Paris with your old man?"

CHAPTER THREE

The sound of my heart is loud in my ears as I rise up through the layers of unconsciousness. My eyelids flicker—bright white light—red inside my eyelids—bright white walls—red inside my eyelids. I force my eyes open and will them to stay that way. I am lying on my back in a small, cold room. My mouth is gagged, and my arms have been pulled up over my head and secured to a metal headboard behind me. Where am I? Why am I . . . ? The memories rush in like a tidal wave. Trees, dirt, and road flying upward in a catastrophe of noise . . . Mum. Addy!

I try to move, but the plastic cuffs are tight, and they eat into my skin. Gray squares blur my vision and I have to lie still for a few moments, sucking in as much air as I can around the fabric that's been stuffed into my mouth, to keep from passing out again. My tongue aches from pulling it far back in my mouth to avoid touching the fabric. I must have been doing this even while unconscious. I want to cry, but I am not going to let myself, because that will mean they've won. Whoever they are.

But of course I already know: the AFC. The extremists who shot my dad.

And I realize it's happened again. All it takes is one lucky shot, one tiny security breach, for everything you love to be ripped away from you. Well, this is the second lucky shot. A momentary anger washes over me. Where the hell were the security forces? How did this happen again? Then I am so overcome with fear that my brain short-circuits, and for a few seconds I think nothing at all until one image forces its way through. A slab of meat no longer recognizable as a human lying still and bloodied on a white tiled floor. I don't know if this is something I have seen in a film or on the news, or if it's just the worst thing my imagination can conjure up. Either way, I know with absolute certainty that these people are going to hurt me, torture me . . . kill me even, to get what they want.

Panic rises up from my belly and explodes out through my mouth in a scream that is muffled by the gag. I wrench my arms forward and arch my back at the same time to get maximum pull, to try and break the plastic ties. The pain in my wrists is excruciating. I let myself drop down onto the bed, still whimpering, sucking in mouthfuls of cold air as my vision blanks again and then slowly clears. I need to calm down. Fainting is not going to help me or Addy or Mum. They need me. I can't afford to fall apart. I have to get out of here; I have to find them. I have to save them.

I force myself to lie still through ten counts. Inhale. Exhale. Inhale.

My name is Robyn Elizabeth Knollys-Green.

I am sixteen years old.

I am the daughter of Stephen Knollys-Green, the prime minister.

I am still alive.

I intend to keep it that way. I repeat the words over and over in my head, until I feel calmer. Then I look about me. The room is small, with white walls and a white tiled floor. A bare bulb burns above me. There is only one window: a high slit up on the wall opposite the bed. There's a single door and, aside from a small wooden chair and the bed I am lying on, no other furniture.

I test my bonds again, clenching my jaw against the pain. The cuffs are secure and tight about my wrists. There is no way that I could get them free without help. That panicky feeling threatens to overwhelm me again. . . . *Focus, Robyn. Inhale. Exhale.*

My legs are unbound. That is good. It means I can kick, and run, if the opportunity arises. My left knee twinges as I bend it, but otherwise my legs move easily. I flex each muscle and joint in turn, working all the way up my body. My focus slips a couple of times, but I drag the air down into my lungs, burying the fear and the panic deep below my rib cage. Aside from the pain in my knee and wrists, some deep scratches to my calves, and a thumping headache, I am okay. I have all four limbs and my head is still attached to my body. These are good things.

As I stretch, I listen. At first I hear nothing beyond my own breathing. Then I begin to pick up small noises: a rustle from the window, a short, high-pitched cry of a bird, the scrape of wood on wood—a chair being pushed back, maybe—and then finally the stamp of a boot on a hard floor somewhere above my head. It is followed by another hard tread and another. Louder. Coming closer.

Seven more thuds, rhythmical and steady. Someone walking down stairs. There is a scratching sound somewhere just beyond my room. I hold my breath. Is someone coming . . . ? Please, don't let . . . I hold my breath as I try to grasp any sound. A thud, farther off. They are moving away. . . . Then five quick slaps, and a clink of a key in the lock, and the door to my room is wrenched open.

Heavy footsteps cross the cell. Then a man's eyes stare down at me from behind a balaclava. His mouth is visible, and a tongue peeps out of rotten yellowed teeth like a slug slithering from rocks. His breathing is fast; his breath smells like something burned to death inside him. His whole body stinks of dankness, mold, and sweat. It is the man who kidnapped me. The one who threatened me with a knife. Not the green-eyed one who caught me.

Sweat gathers in the hollow of my back as I realize how

vulnerable I am. This man could do anything to me down here and no one would know. No one would ever find me.

"You're prettier than you look in your photos, Princess," he says, pulling the gag from my mouth.

I scream as he runs a finger along my hairline and down my cheek. There is something wrong with his finger: there are seams and ridges where smooth skin should be. As if reading my mind, he pulls away so I can see that there is a half-inch cut on the tip of each finger that has then been sewn together with thick black thread. "Fingerprints are tracers. Without them, I'm no one," he explains.

Now is not the time to suggest that what he's actually done is create the world's most unique fingertips. But that's good. That may help me to identify him if—*when*—I get out of here. Even though I can't see his face, he wouldn't be hard to pick out of a crowd. His eyes are dark brown—nothing so unusual there—but he is also the largest man I have ever seen, with broad shoulders and muscles threatening to break free of his tight T-shirt. His arms are veiny, and it occurs to me that he might be on steroids.

He grips my throat, squeezing the air out of me, and then his mouth is so close to my ear that his tongue flicks inside as he whispers in a singsong tone, "No one can hear you."

There is a *clunk* of the door opening, and then a voice says, "What's going on, Scar?"

A man, also in a mask, is standing in the open doorway.

He is tall but thin, and his eyes are bright green. I immediately recognize them. He is the man who caught me before I hit my head on the pavement, the one who apologized. After a brief glance over his shoulder, the first man — Scar? Is that a name? Not his real one, surely — turns back to me. Still holding my throat with one hand, he brushes the hair back from my forehead with the other. "Just getting to know our guest."

My head is almost burrowing into the mattress in an attempt to put as much distance between us as possible.

The green-eyed man comes into the cell. "You need to get away from her."

Scar sniggers. "Oh yeah? What are you going to do about it?"

"I'm — I'll —" Green Eyes pauses and stands up straighter. "Feather won't like it."

"Ooh, Feather won't like it," Scar mocks in a singsongy voice again, but he lets go of my neck. I cough as I breathe in, my throat sore.

The men square up to each other, and for a moment, I think there will be a fight. Then Scar laughs and prods Green Eyes in the chest. "You're not worth it," he says, and leaves, knocking into Green Eyes's shoulder as he passes him.

When Scar is gone, Green Eyes cuts the cable ties off my wrists. "Did he hurt you?" he asks. His voice is soft, with large round Os and gentle Rs. It's calming somehow.

I shake my head as I rub the blood back into my hands

and fingers. Outside, a bird chirps. We both automatically look at the window, even though there is nothing to see. "A goldcrest," he says, moving back to let me sit up.

"Where are my mum and Addy? Please." My voice is as fragile as a bruise.

"They're safe. We didn't take them. Only you."

Only me.

"Why?" I rasp.

"Because you're going to help us save the world."

Green Eyes helps me to the bathroom and tells me his name is Talon. "We are named for the Earth," he says. A blindfold is pulled down over my face, but I sense the change in flooring through the thin soles of my Converses. My cell is tiled and slippery. The floor outside is rougher and more solid. Cement, maybe? My feet scuff against its hard covering.

After seven steps, we turn a corner to the right, then take ten more steps. "Here," Talon says, touching me. I flinch, but he is only guiding my hand to a door handle. "Wait until you are inside and the door is shut, and then take off your blindfold." His breath is bringing up the hairs on the back of my neck.

Without the use of my eyes, I fumble with the handle. It turns, and I push the door open and step inside. My arms flap as I try to find the door again to push it shut behind me. Finally I manage it. Then I pull the blindfold up onto my head.

I am in a small and dirty bathroom. The sink is chipped, the bath yellowed, and the tiles stained. The walls drop paint like dandruff, and one corner of the ceiling is black and sagging with water damage. It is freezing cold in here, an icy blast coming from a rectangular hole covered by metal grates just below the ceiling, above the loo. It is too small to crawl through, even if I could get the grating off. There is no window.

I go over to the sink, above which is a tarnished and cracked mirror. A girl with enormous dark eyes, made larger by the intense shadows under them, and waxy skin stares back at me. There is a bruise on my head, and some blood from a cut to my eyebrow has crusted in my hair, which is falling over my face as usual. I turn on the tap, wincing at the pain in my wrists. The plastic cuffs have left matching blackberry-colored circles. I look bad, and it scares me. I've been worried for three months, but always about Dad, or about another shooting. I never thought someone would kidnap me. The thought is so overwhelming that it makes me dizzy.

The water runs brown, but I splash it over my face anyway, rubbing as hard as I can bear at the gash on my eyebrow to clean it. I force myself to concentrate on getting out any grit. My ears are alert the whole time to any noise from behind me. The water is bitterly cold, and I am shaking by the time I have finished. Then I draw in a long gulp of water. It tastes moldy, but I am so thirsty I don't care.

"Are you nearly done?"

Talon's voice makes me jump.

"Yes," I shout. *Don't come in. Please don't come in.*

I turn off the tap slowly. I don't want to go out there again. I need to get away from here. But I am not strong enough to fight those men. I need a weapon. I scan the bathroom again, sighing when I see nothing that can help me. There aren't even any cupboards that might be hiding aerosols or a toilet plunger.

Talon bangs on the door again. "You need to hurry up."

"Please, give me a moment."

I look at the loo. I have to go, and who knows when I'll get another chance. What if Talon comes in? What if Scar comes in? I shiver as I remember the look in his eyes as he held me down on the bed.

A thin shower curtain runs around the bath. I hold it up and shield the toilet a little from the door. And then I pee as fast as I possibly can.

When I am washing my hands in the sink, I notice that there is a tiny crack in one corner of the mirror. A wedge is loose. After wiggling the end of it, the whole thing comes off with a snap, opening a shallow cut on my index finger.

Another pounding on the door. "Come out now."

I open the door. The shard is gripped tightly in my fist.

Talon is angry. "Wear your blindfold." He pulls it down over my eyes, securing it tightly behind my head, but not before I see the stairs behind him. They are about halfway down the corridor; five, maybe six, paces away.

"You took a long time," Talon says.

I don't answer. Head ducked, hair forward to cover my face, I am busy counting my steps. Two. Three. Four. Five. I put my hand out to my right. The wall is slightly damp. Six. Six and a half. Empty space where the wall should be. I'm here. Now's my chance.

Still blindfolded, I slash at him. The glass meets resistance. I push harder. He cries out and lets me go. I rip the blindfold off. He is leaning against the wall, blood gushing from around the piece of glass that is stuck fast in his arm. I fly up the stairs two at a time and out into a kitchen at the top of the landing, where Scar is sitting at the table, drinking from a mug.

We stare at each other for a second. Then he is running at me, his mug smashing to the floor. I dart sideways, ducking under his arm and spinning around the table. I reach the door at the other end of the room and grab the handle.

I get no farther. Arms come around my chest like straps, tugging me backward. I am still holding on to the door handle, but my grip is slipping. Scar is too strong. Then I realize that maybe I can use his strength against him. Waiting until I feel him tugging back on me with everything he has, I suddenly let go of the door handle. The momentum sends us both crashing to the floor. I try to make myself as heavy as possible, forcing my bony elbows back just as we land, so that they pummel him in the chest, winding him. While he is still dazed, I scramble to my feet and run for the door again. My hands are sweaty and fumbling, and it takes a second longer than it should to tug the door open. I can hear Scar standing up behind me. A scream rises in my throat but I push it down, darting through the open door and then shutting it behind me as fast as I can.

There is a key in the lock on this side. It is the first piece of luck I've had. I hold my breath and I turn the key, willing it to work. There is a click as the bolt locks into place.

The dimly lit corridor beyond the kitchen stretches off in both directions. I have no idea which way I should go. Where would they be keeping Mum and Addy? I don't believe that they're not here. Why would the terrorists take only me, when they could take the PM's whole family? The basement is the obvious answer, but I can't go back there now. If they are down there, their best hope is for me to escape and raise the alarm. I dart down the right branch, praying that it is the way out.

It isn't. The hall twists and turns, becoming darker and darker until it ends in a large room. A sheet of metal has been nailed over the one window, but I can just make out lumps of what must be furniture. It's all been covered with sheets that glow ghostly white in the gloom. Weaving quickly between everything, I try tugging on the metal sheet. It's been secured by a nail in each corner and another one, halfway up each side. I can get my fingers underneath it, but I'm not strong enough to do much more than that. The metal makes a dull *thwack* as I slam my palms against it in frustration. It's drowned out by the louder sound of splintering wood coming from farther down the corridor. There is a roar of triumph. Scar has escaped his prison.

For a second my legs turn to water as fear pushes all the energy out of me like air from a punctured balloon. Then I think of Addy trapped here somewhere. I can't give up so easily. I will not let these people win. *Move, Robyn. Move now!* I need somewhere to hide. The dust sheets, of course. I press myself close to what feels like a sofa and let the sheet drop around me.

Footsteps smack along the corridor, getting more distant. I sigh in relief. He's gone the other way. Perhaps he won't find me here. Maybe if he goes upstairs, I can sneak out and try to find another way out. More footsteps, lighter this time. Talon maybe? He's much smaller than Scar. Then I hear someone moving around overhead. Have they both gone upstairs? Or is there someone else here? I'm so busy listening to the noise above me that it takes a second to realize the light in the room has shifted. Someone must have turned on the light in the corridor.

"Here, kitty kitty. Here, puss, puss." It's Scar.

I can hear him moving around. And I can smell him.

Then the outline of him comes into view. He is crouching down and lifting up the sheet opposite me. I am not even breathing now, and I'm pressed as tightly as I can be against the sofa, wishing I could disappear into it. He lets the dust sheet drop back into place and disappears out of my sight line. The idea of him grabbing me from behind makes the hairs on the back of my neck stand on end. His smell is all around me now, choking me. He must be right above me. I imagine every second that he is lifting the sheet. Is that air I can feel at my back? Has he lifted my sheet? Is he about to find me? Any moment now his big fat hand will be reaching for me—

"Scar!" The sound of Talon's voice comes from upstairs. Then again, more urgently. "Scar!"

Scar grunts. He is leaving the room. The door slams shut behind him.

I let my breath go a capillary at a time, imagining the tiny air particles bubbling up from my lungs and out through my mouth. Still I don't move. I wait and I wait and I wait under that sheet until my legs are cramped and my left foot is completely numb. The world grows darker and darker. The house is silent now. I know that they can't have stopped looking for me, but I have to move. I am beginning to shake with cold. I can't stay here forever. I have to try to get away. I slowly straighten out my legs, one after the other. The house remains quiet, so, with the help of the sofa, I stand up. Then

I move slowly in the dark to avoid knocking anything over. After sidestepping along the wall until I feel the metal sheeting at my back, I put my hand out in front of me. I can't see anything. My fingers brush against something. It is not a sofa or a table. It is silky smooth. Like . . . like hair.

A lamp is switched on and reveals a woman sitting on the other sofa. She is staring at me with dark eyes. A mask covers her face but stops at her neck. My hand is looped in the long dark hair that falls below it.

I scream.

CHAPTER FOUR

"My name is Feather," the woman says. Her voice is as soft as water lapping over pebbles, and in my mind I see the beach near my grandparents' house and remember how suddenly the gentle tide can turn, cutting you off from the shore.

We are in my cell. She's crouching, her back against the locked door. She led me here alone, a gun pushed into the base of my spine. We passed Scar coming out of one of the rooms farther along the corridor. He made a move, to grab my arm or lift me up, but after a glance at Feather, his hands fell back to his sides.

She is small, barely five feet tall. Unlike the others, her balaclava also covers her mouth and nose, meaning only her eyes are visible. They are huge and dark with long, thick eyelashes. They should be beautiful, but there is something in them, like a hidden current in a still river, that makes me think people have been fooled by her gender and her height in the past and have regretted it. My fear grips me more firmly as I remember how she had managed to enter that room and sit there in the dark so silently that I had no idea she was even there. She must have come in after Scar left.

The gun rests on her lap, its barrel still pointed at me. She strokes it absently as she continues, "It is under my instruction that you were brought here."

I am too afraid to speak. Her eyes look ready to swallow me up.

"You are here to help us. Your father has something we want, and you are going to get it for us. As long as you're obedient and your father cooperates quickly, you will not be hurt. But you will do what I say, and you will not try to escape again."

"You're part of the group that shot my dad." I sound small and young and scared.

"You don't get to ask questions. You are not in Number Ten now with your servants and your mummy and your daddy," she says. "You are here, under my rule. I am your route out of here, Princess. Do not piss me off." She lunges forward and clouts me around the ear with the base of the gun. The pain is a firework exploding in my head. "That is for attacking my comrades." She cuffs the other ear—"That is for running"—and my vision clouds. The sizzling in my ears has become a single high-pitched note, like the sound a heart machine makes when someone dies.

I'm tied to the bed again. My arms are aching from being forced over my head. I spent a long time trying to squeeze my hands though the cable ties, but they are too tight, so all I've ended up doing is hurting my wrists more. I am lying still, trying to listen for any sound that might give me a clue as to where I am. It's late now, and a thin orange glow filters through the high window. There must be a light outside. A streetlamp, maybe, or just a security light? Should I shout? Someone might hear me. Gordon once told me that if I was ever in trouble, I should shout "FIRE!" "Help" is too vague, but people know what to do about a fire, so they aren't afraid to get involved. I don't want to shout now, though. The wrong person might come. I can't get the image out of my head of Scar holding me down on the bed.

There's a shriek from outside, and I jump, yanking painfully against my cable ties. Just a fox. I hear them in the garden at Number 10 sometimes. Can Addy and Mum hear this fox? Where are they? Why couldn't these arseholes have kept us together? Addy will be so terrified and tired. It must be way past her bedtime. She'll be crying, and Mum won't be able to calm her down. It's always Karen who puts Addy to bed, and she always, always has her toy lamb to cuddle. She can't sleep without it. She's only three years old. It's not fair. Why couldn't they have left her alone? Why couldn't they have left *me* alone?

The light outside goes off suddenly, and the room is plunged into an impenetrable blackness, extinguishing everything. There's a sound from the corridor like a boot scraping against wood. Who is that? Out of all of them, I hope it's Talon. He seems the most sane.

There's another sound of a footfall. I imagine the door handle turning, even though I can't see it in the dark. I am beginning to feel panicky. I need to calm down. I try to focus on a nice memory. Of last Christmas at Granny and Grandpa's, opening our presents in the hall under the big tree and Mum telling Addy that she should be grateful for what she'd gotten this year. "Some little girls don't have any presents." Addy hugged her new teddy bear to her chest, eyes wide, like she was afraid one of those little girls might try to take it from her.

The memory doesn't last. How could the attack have happened this afternoon? Everyone kept telling me we were safe, but we weren't, and I *knew* it. Why didn't anyone listen to me? I've been afraid since January, and now it feels like it was all leading to this. I am angry and scared, but I have to keep faith in Dad. I know that he will be doing everything he can to bring us home. We won't be here long. Dad will be raising hell at Downing Street to get us out of here. We just have to hold on.

Hold on. Keep calm.

The darkness wraps itself around me until I can no longer remember what it is like to see, and it just seems to go on and on and on and on until I begin to lose all sense of everything. I keep opening my eyes without realizing I've closed them and feeling bad because I've fallen asleep for a few minutes, when I should be awake and plotting how to get out of here and how to rescue Addy and Mum.

I open my eyes suddenly, not even sure when I shut them. Was I sleeping? What woke me? A scream. Addy screaming. Her short, sharp cries were reverberating off the walls of my cell. I try to sit up, remembering too late that I am still tied to the bed. I fall backward, flopping about like a fish. Addy's cries have died down now, and everything is quiet again; even the ringing in my ears has dropped to a low hum. I yell, an incoherent string of noises that definitely has the words "help," "sister," and "bastards" mixed in, along with a few other swear words.

As the locks on the door pull back, I realize how stupid I've been. What if it's Scar?

"Where is my sister? What have you done to her?" I say with more bravado than I feel. The glare of the flashlight is blinding and I look away, green and orange and blue circles dancing before my eyes. When I look back, Talon is beside the bed.

"She isn't here."

"Why should I believe you?"

"Because I'm telling the truth."

"Why are we here?"

"There's no 'we.' There's just you."

"I want to see my sister." The lightbulb swings gently

above our heads, blown by an invisible breeze, casting shadows on the wall in the fierce glare of the flashlight.

"She isn't here."

My throat burns with the effort of not crying. "Please," I murmur, "please let me go."

I notice that he is favoring his left hand. His right arm must be sore from where I stabbed him earlier. Good. I'm glad I hurt him. I would do it again. He swings the flashlight, and I imagine my eyes glowing red in its beam like a woodland animal caught in a car's headlights. He lowers the light so that it is no longer blinding me and says, "I get that you're scared, but we're not going to hurt you. We just need your help. Then you can go home."

"And if I don't help you?"

He shrugs, making his shadow huge and shapeless like a bear. "Then we can't let you go."

There is a media blackout surrounding our trip to Paris, so there weren't the usual hordes of press outside Downing Street and at Northolt airfield. We boarded the Royal Squadron plane quickly and quietly, and it took off almost immediately. We are now somewhere over the Channel. I peer out of the window at the white clouds and try to imagine the strip of sea somewhere far below.

"How are you doing, Robyn?" Gordon, part of the special protection branch of the police and the person in charge of

CHAPTER FIVE

Eventually dawn leaks into the room, scraping back the darkness with her long, thin fingers to the trill of morning birdsong. I didn't hear Addy crying again in the night, but that doesn't mean she isn't here somewhere. I don't believe Talon. I don't have tons of experience with kidnappers, but they aren't known for their open and frank exchanges with prisoners. I'd say they pretty much tell you whatever it is they want you to know.

A little while after sunrise, Talon brings me breakfast. He is more cautious today, untying only one of my wrists, so I'm still fastened to the bed but can sit up to eat. I couldn't attack him now anyway. After last night's restlessness, my muscles feel drained, and my legs and arms are as heavy and inanimate as a wooden puppet's.

His face is still masked, only those vivid green eyes—the color of verdigris on copper—are visible. They never look at me directly. Even as he unties me, he keeps his focus somewhere around my chin level, like maybe he's ashamed or something. As though he thinks that by not looking at me, this might not be happening. It reminds me of Addy's invisibility game, where she walks around my room, eyes half closed, stealing my lip gloss or earrings or other shiny things. When I ask her what she's doing, she says, "I not here. You can't see me. I invisibubble." Thinking about my sister hurts.

Talon left the tray on the chair while he undid the cable ties, but now he puts it next to me on the bed. I notice that he is still favoring his left arm. "Breakfast," he says, like I might be a bit stupid. A newspaper is folded up next to it. I catch sight of the headline as he pushes the tray toward me: PM'S DAUGHTER TAKEN HOSTAGE.

I hesitate, not wanting to give him the satisfaction of having brought me something I actually want, and then the need to know overwhelms me and I snatch it up greedily. There is a grainy photo of me taken at Mum's birthday last year. I wish they had chosen another picture. I am not even smiling in this one. I look stuck up and smug. My long hair is pulled back in a ponytail; my bangs are in my eyes as usual.

Robyn Knollys-Green, the prime minister's sixteen-year-old daughter, was kidnapped shortly after one p.m. yesterday, when the car she was traveling in was ambushed following a roadside bomb just outside Northampton. Security forces have refused to comment on whether there is any link between the kidnapping and the shooting of the prime minister in January, the crime for which Kyle Jefferies is awaiting trial.

Special Operations Driver John McNally is in serious but stable condition. Two other police officers are being treated for minor injuries, while the PM's wife and younger daughter escaped with only cuts and bruises and are recovering at Downing Street.

No organization has yet claimed responsibility for the attack.

Addy and Mum are at Downing Street. They're safe. A horrible thought occurs to me. "You could have made this up. Created it on the computer or something."

"I could have"—he pushes the tray of food toward me—"but I didn't." His eyes flick up to mine for the first time. "Your mum and sister are safe, which is more than I can say for my family."

"What do you mean?"

"Nothing. Just eat."

I ask if he plans on watching me, only I don't say it like that. I ask very politely, in a pathetically small voice, if he could perhaps sit a little bit farther away, if he wouldn't mind very much. Because he is making me really nervous. I don't say that last part either, though.

He doesn't answer, but he does go and lean against the door, which is about as far away as he can get while still being in the room.

I pick up a piece of toast. My mum and sister are safe. They are at home. But that means . . . I put the slice back down. I am here alone. No one beyond my kidnappers knows where I am. Suddenly I don't feel so much like eating. After poking at the things on the tray—a cup of tea, two slices of toast, and a cherry yogurt—I decide I definitely won't be able to eat them. I push the food away.

"Loads of starving kids would be grateful for that food."

I don't answer.

"If you're not going to eat, I'm going to tie you up again." He is wary as he moves toward me. I make my limbs as floppy and heavy as I can when it comes to tying me up. He seems uncomfortable, like maybe he knows this is wrong. At one point, I swear his hands are shaking. In any case, it takes him a long time to fasten the cable ties around the bed.

When he's done, I ask how long I'm going to be here.

"Until your dad cooperates."

I ask what they want, and his eyes shine brightly like there's a sudden fire behind them. Talon clearly cares a great deal about the reason I am here.

"Justice." He says the word slowly and precisely. "I'm not supposed to talk about it. I'm just meant to bring you food and take you to the bathroom. Feather's the one who should be explaining things. She's in charge."

That doesn't fill me with confidence. I have seen a light in Feather's eyes too, but there is something too bright about it. It is a beam that is closer to fanaticism than passion, and besides, so far all she's done is threaten me.

Paris is leached of color. Buildings, trees, gates, people—they are all black smudges on a white background. The city's ice-clenched roads are mostly empty, since few will brave the cold, and the Eiffel Tower is crouched amid the white emptiness like a spider in its web. Just like in Henri Cartier-Bresson's photos.

Dad hadn't been keen on venturing out, but I'd insisted. I know how quickly he can get sucked into things, and I had wanted to keep him to myself as long as possible. A mad walk from the hotel to the Eiffel Tower in the burning cold seemed just the thing, but the tips of my toes are frozen now, even in my sturdy black boots, and I wish I'd put on another pair of tights and remembered my gloves. I took a few photos on the way over here, but my fingers are too cold to take any more. I shrink down farther into my coat, wrapping my scarf once more around my neck.

"The tower's height varies something like ten or fifteen centi-meters, depending on the weather," Dad says, coming up behind me. "'The frost performs its secret ministry.' Here"—he hands me a plastic cup of hot chocolate—"drink this before I have to

phone your mother and tell her you've caught pneumonia."

"You can't catch pneumonia," I say, "only the infections that cause it."

"Where did you learn to be so pedantic?"

"I wonder. . . ."

And he gives a belly laugh like Father Christmas in the Coke adverts. I can't remember the last time I heard him laugh like that. His hair is thinner now; it starts farther back on his forehead, and I am sure there are more creases around his eyes. Running the country has made my dad old.

I take a sip of my hot chocolate. "How tall is it then, the tower? Come on. I know you're dying to tell me."

"Three hundred twenty-four meters or one thousand sixty-three feet, roughly equivalent to an eighty-one-story building. Built in 1889, it was the tallest building in the world for forty-one years until the Chrysler Building—"

"Yes, thank you, Dad. The important question is, can we climb it? And the answer to that is yes." But Dad's face is not saying yes. It's saying, I have a meeting with the French president on Thursday to discuss Anglo-Franco trade agreements and a mountain of reports to read before then. *"It's okay," I say. "Another time. We probably wouldn't see much today with all the clouds anyway."*

"The summit on Thursday with the president is very important, but that doesn't mean I don't want to make the most of our time here," he says.

So long as it doesn't interfere with any planning. "Are you nervous about the meeting?"

"Me? Nervous? No way, kiddo."

I roll my eyes. "'Kiddo'?"

"Not what all the kids are saying these days?"

"No, Dad. Stick to being a boring old politician in a gray suit, all right? Seriously, though, do you ever get nervous?" *He has met so many leaders and dictators over the years. Sometimes I am too scared to even read aloud in English class.*

"Sometimes. But it's practice mainly, and preparation. And remembering that people are just people. Even the scary ones. I do like to be ready, though. It is so much easier to get people on board if you understand one another. And unity is even more important now that the world is in such flux. There are a lot of angry people out there, Bobs. It's important to shore up relationships. Not everyone agrees with the way other nations conduct themselves. It's my responsibility to ensure that no one can find fault with Britain."

"You're talking like a politician."

"Am I?"

"Dad, the fire at Bell-Barkov last year . . ."

"What on earth has put that into your head now?"

"On the plane Gordon said something about a security breach, and I've heard people saying that the AFC are angry with you because of something to do with Michael."

"The AFC are terrorists."

"But you're not in danger or anything, are you?"

"Me? Goodness, no. Nothing is going to happen to me."

Gordon, who had been talking on his mobile, comes up to us then and says that we should be getting back.

"We'll talk about this more later," Dad says to me, before beginning to walk back toward the main road with Gordon.

Irritation bubbles inside me, making the hot chocolate taste sour in my mouth. I was talking to Dad. Why does everyone always have to interrupt? Why are their questions always more important than mine? We won't talk about this later. We never do talk properly.

Gordon and Dad are walking a little ahead of me now, with Gordon laughing at something Dad has said. I drop back farther, watching my boots turn white to black to white as I drag my feet through the snow. Dad stops to wait for me, throwing his arm around my shoulder as soon as I get close enough. I shrug him off, sidestepping out of reach. I am rewarded by seeing a flash of annoyance in his eyes. Good. Now he knows how it feels to be disappointed. It is childish, and I immediately regret it when Dad stalks off without a word. I want to call out that I am sorry, that I just want to spend more time with him—but something in the set of his shoulders keeps me silent.

Dad is standing over my bed when I wake up. It must be early evening, as his face is an inkblot in the thin light from the high-up window. A gasp catches in my throat. They have found me!

"Dad!" I say, tears welling in my eyes as my arms go around his neck. He holds me close, and I breathe in the familiar musky scent of his aftershave and the traces of cigar smoke. "How did you find me?" I cling to him more tightly.

"We're going to get you out of here. There are police everywhere. You're safe now. You're safe."

I open my eyes. The cell is flooded with sunlight; the window is a splice of pale blue. Dust particles dance in the sparkling light, pirouetting in a golden line from the window to the opposite wall of the cell, where they seem to converge into shapes. It is like looking into a kaleidoscope.

Dad isn't here. No one is but me. It was just a dream. I wasn't even asleep. It's too uncomfortable with my hands pulled over my head. I think I just passed out for a while, which is annoying, as I'd been trying to keep track of time. How much darker is it in here now than before? Was I out for ten minutes, twenty, an hour? I have no idea.

The light from the window disappears, taking the frolicking dust particles with it. A spider scuttles across the bare wall toward the door. I watch as it crawls through a crack in the door frame. My mouth tastes like a trash can, and a headache is pushing at my eyes. I must have been sweating in my sleep, because my hair is stuck to my face in clumps. I can't even push it away.

Outside, a bird is crying a thin, high note. *Zi-zi-zi. Zi-zi-zi.* I imagine the view outside: a garden, an oak tree, birds. Beyond, what? A hill? A forest? Fields? The image is replaced with another: the Eiffel Tower through my camera lens, looking black and spindly, and standing tall in a world of ice and frost.

I force the memory away and instead imagine the Downing Street garden. The trees arch over my head, corseting the blue sky. Addy is running, screaming with laughter, because Poppy is chasing her.

My wrists are so sore. I want to sit up, just for a little bit. Maybe if I shout? I'm afraid that Scar will come, but I'm more afraid that my hands will drop off soon if I don't get the blood circulating. I call out, quietly at first, and then louder. Eventually the door opens and Talon comes in. The second I see him, I beg for him to untie me, knowing it's degrading, but I don't care. It's not like he doesn't know who has the power here. "I won't hurt you," I add, when his hand goes unconsciously to the stab wound on his arm. "Please, I just have to move. Just a couple of minutes."

Finally he comes over to the bed and begins to cut the cable ties from my wrists. Just as he is fiddling with the second tie, the door bangs open again. "What the hell is going on?" Feather asks. Then, as she takes in the scene in front of her, she yells, "You untied her!"

"She was in pain."

"I don't care. She tried to escape."

One of my arms has gone to sleep, and it flops about in my lap. I shake it hard to get some feeling back into it. Talon eyes me for a second, to make sure that I'm not about to attack him, and then goes to Feather.

She is clearly furious, but she lowers her voice as she goes on about how everything they have done will be pointless if I escape. "She is our last chance! You'd better not be backing out on me, because—"

"This means as much to me as it does to you, but I don't see any reason to make this harder on her than it has to be," Talon assures her.

"You are lucky Talon is so compassionate," she says to me. "If it were my choice, your hands would stay tied up until your arms dropped off."

She doesn't tie me up again, though. That makes me think that Talon must have some influence. Maybe that's something I can play on? He is definitely the kindest of my kidnappers. Can I convince him to help me?

I have been pacing the cell since they left me. It feels good to move around, and it's easier to think when I'm not tied up. I'm back to keeping track of time, watching very carefully for shifts in the sunlight. It's getting dark now, so I reckon it must be about eight o'clock. Talon has left one of the cable ties attached to the bedpost, so I pull it off and experiment by dragging it down the wall. If I press hard enough, I can make an indent in the plaster. Then, because I don't want my kidnappers to know what I'm doing, I crawl under the bed and begin to work the tie up and down against the wall. Two marks. One for yesterday, when I was brought here, and one for today. The scratches look like the beginning of a fence. I imagine it running around the four walls, not just once, but twice, three times, four. A wall of little fences. I won't be here that long, though, I tell myself. Dad is coming for me.

I roll out from under the bed and sit down on it. Then, to distract myself, I create a viewfinder with the thumb and index finger of one hand and circle it around the room, looking for a good shot. White walls, white ceiling, white floor, a tiny slice of window. I let my hand drop. I don't want to take a photo of anything in here. Photography for me is about memories, and there is nothing in here that I want to remember. Before I can stop it, the familiar refrain starts up in my head again. *Come on, Dad. Find me. Please. Bring me home.*

I have no appetite. I don't know if it's sickness or fear, but once again, I ignored the food Talon brought me for breakfast. He didn't comment on it this time, just took me to the bathroom. I swill the toothpaste around my mouth and spit it out in the cracked sink in the bathroom. (I have been given a toothbrush, toothpaste, soap, and a small hand towel. Thank goodness.) Then I flush the toilet and wash my hands and face. I know that I stink, but I won't take off my clothes to wash without a lock on the door. I haven't seen Scar since that first day—it is always Talon who brings me my food and takes me to the bathroom—but I know Scar is still here. I hear his voice sometimes, coming from the room above me.

After drying my face with the towel—I have to stop several times to clutch the sink and breathe deeply because I think I will vomit—I open the door to the bathroom. Feather is leaning against the wall. "Talon says you're not eating. Why? Don't you like the food?"

"I . . . I can't eat. I think I'm sick."

"Nonsense." But her eyes travel over my face again, assessing. "You'll die if you don't eat. We didn't bring you here to die." She scratches at her neck under her mask, as though the wool is irritating her skin. She has a different one on today, one with a cutout for her mouth. She is speaking again, but I don't hear the words. I am fascinated by the movement of her mouth: the flash of white teeth, the tip of a ruby tongue, the rosy flush of her lips. The colors are so bright against the black mask. I lean forward, tilting my head. Her mouth is a shell and her tongue a sea snake, the deep darkness of her throat its home. The snake darts out of its cave, jet-black eyes watching me.

"Robyn!"

The snake flicks back into its hole, becomes a tongue again in a pink mouth full of tiny white teeth.

"Robyn." She hauls me into a sitting position. Somehow

I am on the floor. My forehead is tender as if I have hit it against something. I am watching Feather's mouth again: open, close, open, close. The muscles in her jaw contract and expand. Contract. Expand.

Now the floor is moving and somehow I am above it, suspended in the air. I look down. My legs are moving, my feet scrabbling to grip the slippery floor. Just before I black out, I see that someone is holding me up. Then—

I can't breathe. My nose, my eyes. Clogged. I can't see. I draw a breath and cough and gasp—and rise up to the surface. I splutter until I am finally able to draw a lungful of air. I pull in another one. In front of me is a white face. Gray eyes. It takes a second to realize that I am back in the bathroom and looking at myself in the cracked mirror. The sink below me is full of water. Feather is holding the scruff of my T-shirt as though preparing to give me another dunking. Seeing that I am conscious again, she lets go and steps away from me. "You kept fainting," she says, as if that is a reason to nearly drown someone.

I breathe in slowly a few more times as she sits down on the edge of the bath. "No one wants you to die," she says. "That isn't part of the plan."

This seems a little ironic, given that a few seconds ago she was holding my head in a sink full of water, but I say nothing. When my head and lungs are clearer, I turn to face her, gripping the sink behind me, to offer some support in case I feel dizzy again.

"What do you want to eat?" she asks.

"I don't know. I can't." I woke up feeling ill this morning. Day three, and I'm ill. Maybe it was the water I drank from the sink on the first day?

"You can't get sick and you can't die." She stands up as if that is an end to it.

She leads me back to the cell, her arm supporting my elbow. There is a cheese sandwich on a paper plate on the floor next to a plastic beaker of water. She nods at it. "Eat." Again—"*Eat!*"—when I hesitate. The bread is soft and fresh, but the taste of toothpaste is still in my mouth and bile rises after only a single bite. Feather is watching me and I swallow it, breathing through clenched teeth.

She stays with me, sitting silently, until I have forced the whole sandwich down. "You know, animals in the labs at Bell-Barkov wouldn't be treated with the same respect," she says, handing me the beaker of water. "If one of them got sick because they refused to eat, it would be put down and another animal brought in to replace it. Animal life is cheap to humans."

I don't know how to respond to that, so I don't answer. I'm the one being kept in the cage here.

"What do you know about animal testing?" she continues without giving me a chance to talk. "Nothing, I'm guessing. Do you know whether the drugs you take, the makeup you wear, are tested on animals? Do you even *care*?"

She stands up. "You're just like the majority of people in this country. No one gives a shit about the planet. Well, they need to be *made* to care. Violently, if necessary. People are so stupid. We're trying to make a difference, and what do they do? Lock us up for crimes we didn't commit, just to get us off the streets."

"Please," I ask, "what does this have to do with me?"

"You're human, aren't you? You *live* on this planet?" She laughs nastily. "If what you mean is what does it have to do with you being here, in this cell, then say so. Well? Is that what you mean?"

I nod. "What—what do you want?"

"I want many things. An end to all animal testing in the UK. I want them to stop drilling in the Arctic Ocean. I want no more deforestation. There is so much I want for this planet, but my priority right now is to secure the immediate release of Kyle Jefferies, or Marble as he is known to his family and friends." Her eyes are jet-black in the bright light. "You want to go home, Princess? You get my brother freed."

CHAPTER SIX

Mum calls as soon as Dad gets back to the hotel. I've barely had a chance to say hello to him. So much for some time, just him and me. Dad sits in the desk chair, and I pull up a chair of my own. He puts the phone on speaker and props it up against his briefcase, so we can both talk into it. I don't say much.

"Are you having a good time?" Mum asks.

"Bobs nearly caught pneumonia today," Dad says, with a wink at me.

Mum misses the joke and takes it as an opportunity to worry. "You need to wrap up, darling. Make sure you wear your scarf tomorrow. Stephen, make sure she does."

"Yes, sir," Dad says as I roll my eyes.

"How's Addy?" I ask before Mum insists I start wearing thermal underwear.

"Itchy," Mum says. "What have you two done today, then? You're not very talkative, Robyn. Tell me all about Paris. Wish I was there, rather than stuck in the Goldfish Bowl." It's what Mum calls Number 10. "Seventeen journalists by the gates

this morning. Seventeen! Really, don't they have something more important to report than whether I wore the red Burberry jacket rather than the blue?"

Dad laughs.

"It isn't funny, Stephen. I am sick of this. Sick of it!"

"Well," Dad says somberly, "take comfort. At this rate, we won't win the next election."

"Oh, don't be ridiculous. Of course you will," Mum replies in a tone that implies that dreams—hers, at least—do not come true.

To deter Parental Armageddon, I tell her about the Eiffel Tower and then about the underground catacombs Gordon took me to this afternoon while Dad was in a meeting. The tombs were full of skulls arranged in all sorts of patterns and shapes.

"Sounds absolutely hideous," Mum says. "Good grief, Stephen, couldn't you have taken her to a gallery or something?" Then she asks about the briefing, saying the deputy prime minister's wife called "in a right flap" about something.

I stop listening. Pushing my chair back, I go to peer out of the window. We're in the small study just off the main living room of the suite. There's no view, only a white wall opposite and a small courtyard ten floors down. For security reasons, we never get a view. All the rooms that overlook the courtyard on this floor and the one above are either empty or occupied by members of our staff.

Mum is still rabbiting on about something completely irrelevant, like what color she should paint the Terracotta Room or did Dad know that the Fitzwilliams are spending the summer on Martha's Vineyard.

Dad is always telling me to make more of an effort with Mum, and I try, but . . . I don't know. It annoys me the way she nags at Dad. I am not the biggest fan of Downing Street, and I find the fact that I am expected to call my own father "Prime Minister" in public ridiculous, but this is who Dad is. And I love him. God, that's cheesy. But I do. Yes, he is embarrassing, and last week he called only the most famous boy band in the world the wrong name in front of the entire nation, and don't even get me started on his dancing—it could start world wars.

Yet he is the prime minister of Great Britain. The decisions he makes every day affect so many people. Not just Britons, but people across the globe. And that is phenomenal. I lie awake at night worrying about whether I'll get an A in my GCSEs while he is deciding how best to deal with North Korea, or China, or the global fiscal crisis, or the NHS, or the benefit system, or . . . brain freeze.

Allowances have to be made for having that level of stuff on your mind. Mum doesn't agree, though, and still goes off on him for leaving his clothes on the floor, or not asking the Scotts to dinner, or not taking me to a gallery in Paris.

I know it's hard for Mum too, though. She hates Downing Street. She likes the parties, but she hates the chitchat and the *constant backstabbing. And the press are always having a go at her. They've spied a chink in Dad's armor, and they stick a knife into it as often as possible. But that annoys me too. Why can't Mum just get it right?*

Dad says I need to have more sympathy. He says me and Addy are her everything. She had four miscarriages before I was born, and then, of course, there was my brother, Robin. He was a stillbirth. Dad says I can't begin to imagine what they went through, especially Mum.

I was born four agonizing years later, after endless rounds of IVF. Dad says Mum called me her "little miracle" and held me for a whole week before she would put me down. I find that hard to imagine now. I always think of my sister as the miracle baby, born to Mum when she was really old with no IVF, no nothing. Adriana is a miracle; I'm the girl who should have been a boy. Is that why Mum and I don't always get along? Has she been disappointed in me since I was born?

I sit back down and rest my legs on the arm of Dad's chair. He rubs my toes absentmindedly, like he used to when I was a kid.

"You stink," Feather says. "You have to take a bath." After making sure I ate my sandwich, she'd left me to rest a bit. I actually fell asleep, amazingly, and I do feel better now. But I still have a fragile, tight-skinned feeling, like even the sheets on the bed might bruise me. I'm hoping the sickness was just tiredness, or fear. I don't want them to be drugging me.

After taking me back to the bathroom, Feather lets the taps run in the bath. They don't bother to blindfold me on trips to the bathroom now. The tub is stained, making the water turn mustard yellow. The thought of sitting in it is not appealing, even if I do smell. My disgust must show on my face, because Feather asks me acidly whether I'd like the butler to clean it first.

After she's gone—"Don't take too long. The makeup assistants are waiting"—I stare at the water spluttering from the tap, imagining taking off my filthy, stinking clothes and sliding down under it, working the soap up into a lather and drawing it up over my arms. I could even wash the grease and blood out of my hair. And on the toilet seat is a pile of clean clothes. A T-shirt, underwear, a pair of tracksuit bottoms, and a navy-blue hoodie. They look warm and comfortable. I desperately want to be clean, and yet something stops me. I am too afraid to take my clothes off and sit in that bathtub. Not because of the stupid yellow water, but because what if someone came in and saw me naked? What if Scar . . . ? I know what was in his mind, when he came to my cell alone, and the thought of what he could have done makes my stomach fist.

But I am afraid of what Feather will do to me if I don't bathe. She held my head under water when I passed out. I can't imagine her having any qualms about holding the rest of me under when I am conscious.

The bath is a quarter full now, so I turn off the tap. *Come on, Robyn. Just do it quickly. Clothes off. In. Dunk. Wash. Out. Clean clothes on.*

I can't. I can't. I can't.

What if I didn't have to take my clothes off? Could I do it then? Feather would hear the water swishing, and I would be a little cleaner when I came out. Before I can analyze this too much, I step fully clothed into the tub. When I sit, my skirt balloons up around me and my BETWEN YOU AND ME T-shirt becomes see-through with the water. But at least I am not naked.

I dunk my head, then grab the soap and lather it over my scalp. I wash quickly, pulling my clothes away from my skin. When I'm done, I clamber out, fabric sticking to me. Feather has already started banging on the door and telling me to hurry the hell up. At the sound of her voice, my hands start shaking, and it is an effort to wrap the towel around me. I remember something the therapist I saw after the shooting in Paris said about breathing from the belly to calm anxiety, so I try it now: sticking my belly out and imagining tugging the oxygen right down into my lungs. In my mind, I go over all the things I know about these people: Scar's slashed fingers, Talon's green eyes, Feather's dark ones and how she is so small. And the most important thing: The reason I am here is because Feather wants her brother, Kyle Jefferies, freed. That means I know her surname as well. Next I remember the layout upstairs and how many steps it is from my cell to the bottom of the staircase. These are all things I can use, if not now, then later. They will either help me escape or they will help the police catch these people.

My hands have stopped shaking. I work my way out of my own clothes and into the new ones. Feather bangs on the door as I am pulling the hoodie over my head.

I am staring dumbly at the red light of a video camera. My cell has been made into a makeshift studio, with a blackout curtain pinned to the window and a lamp angled on my face. On the floor in front of the bed is a sheet of paper with the words I am supposed to have memorized. I can't remember a single one, even though I have spent a long time looking at them. My brain is in panic mode, where it just keeps saying *Remember this, remember this* over and over again, until the words are blurring on the page and adrenaline is surging through me, making my chest hot. I'm getting a tension headache too, and the sick feeling is back. Never mind remembering the words on this page. There's a very real possibility I will throw up all over them.

All three of my kidnappers are here: Talon and Feather by the door, Scar working the camera, his hulking frame bent almost double to be at the same height as the tripod. It is the first time I have seen him since I tried to escape. His eyes still slither over me, and I sense his excitement as he flicks his slimy tongue across his lower lip. There is something else beyond desire in his look now. Anger? No. It is more like resentment; the others don't trust him to guard me anymore. Neither do I. It could be the one thing the three of us agree on.

"What's the matter, Princess?" he scoffs. "Can't read?"

"We're waiting, Robyn," Feather says. She and Talon are standing close together. I wonder how he can stand being so near her.

"I . . . I can't remember all the words."

Feather mutters a series of obscenities at me and about me.

"It's a long speech," Talon interrupts. "Give her time."

"Marble doesn't have time."

"We've time," Talon says quietly, touching her arm. A look of understanding passes between them, and Feather's fingers flex, and relax.

After retrieving the sheet of paper from the floor and holding it out to me, Talon tells me to divide it into sections. "We'll film a bit at a time."

"Won't work. It'll look like shit," Feather says.

He persuades her to just give it a go. "Read the first few paragraphs over to yourself, Robyn, and then we'll record them," Talon says.

I look at the paper, letting my hair fall in front of my face, like it might protect me from them.

Hi, Dad, I read to myself. *I'm safe, but I'm scared and*

I want to come home, even though they're treating me well. My kidnappers want to make it clear that they are not terrorists. They just believe that this sort of decisive action is the only way to bring public attention to their cause. The next few paragraphs are about corporate greed and Bell-Barkov's drug testing program. All the stuff that Feather was talking to me about earlier. I read the page over three more times. Feather is pacing the cell, her fingers beating a rhythm on the wall; Scar sticks his finger in his nose and rummages around, and Talon waits quietly.

"Ready?" he finally asks. His voice is kind. His eyes are gentle; it's as if he really wants me to succeed.

I skim the paragraphs again, and then nod. After smearing the contents of his nose on the wall under the window, Scar grins and presses record. The red light blinks at me again. My mind goes blank. I get as far as the second sentence and falter.

Feather smacks her fist into her palm. The snapping sound makes my stomach turn over.

"I'm sorry. I'm sorry," I say. "I'll try harder. 'Hi, Dad. I'm safe, but—'"

"She needs to do it in her own words," Talon says.

Feather silences him with a wave of her hand. "No. She'll get it muddled. We need to clearly state what we want. The trouble is that she doesn't have enough at stake. We have treated her too well. She thinks we aren't serious. Scar, show the clip."

Scar pulls his phone out of his pocket and shoves it in my face as Talon drops his head, as though ashamed. For a second or two, the camera screen is grainy, and there are blurred shapes that slowly resolve themselves into people and then what I recognize as press photographers and journalists. The image bounces and then refocuses on a sign for the London Clinic. The camera moves down and shows Mum, Dad, and Addy, emerging from the glass double-fronted doors. Mum's arm is in a sling and Addy is clutching at her, little fingers wrapped in her skirt. Her toy lamb is caught tight in her other arm. Dad acknowledges the press with a brief nod of his head and then leads Mum and my sister to the waiting car. The image tightens, cropping off Mum and Dad, to concentrate on Addy. My heart clenches at the sight of her large, scared eyes. There is a bloody scratch just above her right eye. Suddenly she turns her head. Caught dead center in the shot, she seems to be staring right into the camera, but of course she can't be, because she has no idea that she is being watched. Being stalked.

I lunge at Feather, fists flying and legs kicking. I want to hurt her, knock her to the floor and punch her again and again and again until she knows what it's like to be in pain, to be sick and hungry and lonely and tired and more scared that you ever thought possible. She goes down easily, and I manage to land a few feeble smacks to her face and arms before Talon drags me off her. The rage is in me, though, and I am a wild animal, biting and scratching and howling. My hands become claws that tear at his face, my teeth fangs that sink into any bare skin I find. *You will not hurt my sister. You. Will. Not!*

Scar joins in the fight. I elbow him in the nose and then I bite one of his disgusting scarred fingers so deep the tang of blood fills my mouth. He slaps me on the side of the head, making the world somersault. After fumbling at his waist, he draws a knife from his belt—

There's a yell from behind us and we all turn to Feather, who is pointing her gun right at us. "Enough!" she says. "Stand up. All of you. Robyn, your little sister is cute. I imagine she would be terrified if someone were to grab her and bundle her into the back of a van. Read the speech again now. Read it and memorize it. You have half an hour, or else . . ." She snatches the phone from my hand and clicks it off. Addy is swallowed up in darkness.

"On the twenty-eighth of January of this year, Kyle Jefferies—known to his friends as Marble—was forced from his house at gunpoint by six police officers for allegedly shooting you, Dad. Since then he has been remanded in custody and refused bail. If he is convicted, he could face life in prison. But he's innocent! It was all a setup. You have to let him go. My kidnappers are willing to make a deal with you. They will release me when you release Marble. Please, Dad, release

Marble so I can come home. . . ." I stumble to a halt. I am shaking with fear. I can't remember the rest of the speech. An image of Addy being dragged screaming from her bed in the middle of the night or snatched on the street flashes through my mind, and I beg Feather to give me a minute to sort myself out before I finish the recording.

I suck in the stale air of my cell and force the vision of Addy out of my head. At the moment she is at home with Dad and Mum, playing with her toys, stroke-slapping my poor cat, and probably bossing everyone around as usual. She's safe. Now it's up to me to make sure she stays that way.

I don't want Kyle Jefferies released from prison. He is a terrorist. He deserves to be in prison, so that he can never hurt anyone again. But right at this second, it isn't his freedom I'm asking for. It's mine. Dad will know I don't mean what I'm saying, and if he doesn't, because he is too panicked at the thought of what these arseholes might be doing to me, then his team of advisers will tell him. The special-ops police force and MI5 will already be looking for me. It won't take them long to find me. I just need to hang on and to stop these people from going after my sister until then. Dad often says that the end justifies the means. *Sometimes, Bobs, you've got to do whatever it takes to get something done. Use any weapons available to you.* And the weapons at my disposal right now are my kidnappers' own words. I will use them to set myself free and keep my sister safe.

And I make a pact with myself. I am going to survive this. One day I am going to walk free from here, and I am going to see my sister and my parents again. I will do whatever it takes.

The camera light is still flashing. I look deep into its eye, and I speak for Addy and for Mum and for Dad. This time my words are clear and I don't falter. I am speaking Feather's sentences but with my eyes, my lips, my tears, I am saying, *I love you, Addy. I love you, Dad and Mum. I am alive and I am coming home.*

I do the whole speech in one take, and when I look down, I realize that my hands are no longer shaking. I finish with, "The date is the thirteenth of April, and actor Maria Cartwright died today, aged eighty-three."

Feather tells me that the last sentence is to authenticate the tape. It is to mark the date and prove that I'm still alive.

"Good," Feather says when I'm done. "The tears are a nice touch. Now I believe you want to go home. Now I believe you want to save your sister."

Scar dismantles the video equipment. I watch him from my crouched position on the bed. Have I done enough? Is Addy safe?

By the door, Talon and Feather talk in low whispers. Talon says something about there being no mention of Jez. Feather doesn't answer immediately. Instead she scoops up a cable at her feet, unplugs it from the wall, and begins looping it around her forearm. "Marble is our priority for the moment," she says.

"But Jez is dead."

"Exactly! Nothing can hurt him right now, but Marble is in prison! How the hell do you think he's coping with that? You know how fragile he is. As soon as we know that he's going to be released without charge, we'll shift focus to Jez. You'll get your revenge, don't worry."

"I don't care about revenge. I care about the truth," he snaps. After a pause, he says, "Robyn must be thirsty. I'll get her a drink."

"Enjoying his role as nursemaid, that one," Scar snarls when he's gone.

Something about Scar's comment must register with Feather, because she looks at me, a calculating expression on her face.

I shift uneasily. "Will . . . is Addy going to be okay?"

"We'll just have to wait for the critics' verdict on your little performance, won't we?" Feather replies, but she is only half listening, and her eyes have drifted to the door Talon just walked through.

CHAPTER SEVEN

Dad and I are drinking hot chocolate on the Champs-Élysées. This afternoon the sky is blue and the sun is bright. A woman is marching past the café. The baguette in her bag is waving furiously, like it is conducting an invisible orchestra.

"What would you have called me if Robin hadn't died?" I ask.

Dad is silent, so I flake off a piece of pastry and dunk it in my hot chocolate, then ask if we can go to the Fondation Henri Cartier-Bresson museum sometime. I'm hoping for tomorrow

"I thought we were talking about your brother."

I dunk another piece of pastry, letting go this time and watching it disappear beneath the froth. "I didn't think you wanted to."

"You give up too easily. How will I ever make a politician of you? Maybe Katherine, after your grandmother. Maybe Millicent, or Dorothy."

I screw up my face, and he smiles.

"Does it upset you to have your brother's name?"

"No . . . not really. Sometimes. Do you wish I had been a boy?"

"Robyn Elizabeth Knollys-Green, I have been in politics for more years than I care to admit. In that time, I have averted wars, rebuilt an ailing economy, and met more foreign dignitaries than I can count. And yet you and your sister, and your brother, are my proudest achievements. There is nothing about you that I would change."

The sun is bright through the café window. It lights Dad up from behind and makes the gray in his hair shine almost gold. "Never wish things to be different," he says. "It is an impossible task, aside from anything else. And thinking about impossible tasks is rather exhausting. Things are as they are. It is up to us how we handle them. And never apologize for who you are. No"—a smile twitches on his lips—"never apologize period, or at least, not loud enough for anyone to hear you."

"Do you never apologize for anything?"

"No. My thought is and must always be: 'I am able to save this country, and no one else can.'"

"Who said that?"

"William Pitt. The Elder."

"You are always quoting somebody."

"Words are a powerful weapon. A single word can change a destiny. You wouldn't waste a bullet—or a nuclear warhead. Don't waste a word."

I swish my spoon through the last froth of my chocolate.
"Are you able to save this country?"

"I think so."

"And what does everyone else think?"

"Who cares? I am the prime minister. It's true that not
everyone likes the methods I use to run the country, but it's
important to follow your own path. We can't please all the
people, all of the time."

"What methods don't they like? What do you do?"

"Whatever is necessary—" He is cut off by Gordon coming
into the café.

"Prime Minister," he says, "I think we should move on.
There appears to be a man with a camera. . . ."

Gordon is standing in the window, blocking out the sun.
For a second, Dad is in shadow, his features so obscured by
darkness that I almost don't recognize him. Then he stands
up and is illuminated in sunlight again. "Come on, Bobs," he
says. "Carpe diem. Let's go and see more of Paris."

It is just after my afternoon trip to the bathroom on the
fourth day when Talon brings me the book *An Encyclopedia*
of Woodland Birds. It is a pretty unusual choice of reading
material. "It was my dad's. I thought that maybe you'd like to
try to identify the birds outside from their calls," he says, looking almost embarrassed. "The sounds are written out as you
say them, and there are pictures." He flips through a couple

of the pages, and we both look down at the brightly colored (and actually beautiful) photos of various birds. Seeing them makes me yearn for my camera.

"The video you made yesterday was good," he goes on. "I'm sure they'll release Marble very soon, and then you can go home."

I pick at a loose thread in the knee of my tracksuit bottoms. "Have you heard from him? My dad."

"Negotiations are ongoing." He sounds like he's reading a prewritten statement.

"So you are talking to him? He's going to release Kyle Jefferies in exchange for me?"

"As I said, negotiations are ongoing."

So he hasn't agreed, or rather the government hasn't agreed. They must have promised something, though, because I am still alive. My worry must still show on my face, though, because Talon says, "You're the PM's daughter. If you speak out against him, things will change. They'd have to. He couldn't silence you. Not his own daughter. He'd obviously do anything for you."

I fall back on the bed. I've always known that being rescued is my greatest hope of survival, so what the hell are the police waiting for? Couldn't they just bang on the front door of every house in the country until they find the one I'm in? I don't care if that isn't realistic and is some sort of human rights violation. What about my human rights?

"Feather wants you to eat upstairs this evening. She's pleased with the recording but thinks you're still not eating properly." Talon sighs. "This will be over, just as soon as we sort things out with your dad."

I roll over and look at the tiny window.

"'There's a blue sky today," he says, as though reading my mind. "Wispy clouds. There was a jay on one of the bushes out there earlier. There's a picture in the book if you're interested."

"This book really belonged to your dad?"

He looks away, and I know we are both thinking the same thing: Why is he giving his dad's book to his hostage?

"Yeah, and then it was my brother's. Jez was sick a lot when he was a kid. He couldn't go out much, but there was a big tree just outside his window that was always full of birds. Dad gave him that book so he could listen to them and know what they were."

And now Talon is giving that book to me.

Is he beginning to sympathize with me? There was a story in the newspaper a few months back, about a girl who was attacked in the street. Instead of panicking, she started telling the guy about her life: her friends, her favorite food, a book she loved. He let her go without hurting her. Later, the police said it was because she made him see her as a person—someone like him, and not a victim. If Talon sees me like that, will he be less likely to hurt me if something goes wrong with the negotiations?

"There's a big tree in the Downing Street garden," I say quickly. "I climbed it once. Mum nearly had a heart attack. It was great, though. I could see over the wall and all the way across Horse Guards Parade."

"You should think about that tree now. It could be like a piece of home here with you," Talon says.

I pick at the loose thread on my pants again, pretending I'm not imagining myself outside, under that tree in Downing Street, both arms outstretched under an azure sky. Only the tree in my mind is larger than the one at home, and its branches are now loaded with birds.

That evening Talon leads me up from the basement. I'm not blindfolded this time, but of course Talon is still masked. I wonder fleetingly how he and the others are going to eat with their faces covered. The kitchen at the top of the stairs smells of garlic and onion. A pan of tomato sauce is bubbling over on the stove. "Feather!" Talon calls. "The food's burning." I jump, but whether from the suddenness of his cry or because his fingers brush my arm as he gently steers me through the doorway and into the corridor beyond, I can't tell. The door still hangs half off its hinges from when Scar broke it down to come after me.

Feather comes out of a room to the left of the kitchen. She pushes past us. "Go in. Sit down. I'll serve up."

We turn a bend in the hall and there is the front door.

Light from the outside world is spilling through its colored glass panes and making splashes on the tiled floor. If only I had turned left instead of right on that first day. I can't run now; Talon is holding my arm too firmly.

We go into a living room. Scar is slouched on the brown couch, his legs stretched out under the glass table, a pillow stuffed under his head. His mask is half pushed up over his nose. He quickly pulls it down over his chin as we enter, but not before I've caught a glimpse of full lips and a rounded chin.

The TV is on and Feather turns the volume up as she comes in, setting one of the three bowls she is holding on the table and balancing the other two in the crook of her arm. "Yours is in the kitchen, Scar."

She settles on the floor and, after rolling her mask up to her nose, begins to shovel the pasta and sauce into her mouth. Talon hands me a bowl and a plastic fork. He brushes the sofa down with his hand and gestures for me to sit. After I've done so, he lowers himself down beside me, giving Feather, who grins up at him, a playful kick in the back.

Scar comes back with his bowl as the news is starting. I am struggling to eat again. The sauce is more water than tomato, and the pasta sticks to my mouth like wet cement. After only a few mouthfuls, I put the fork down and let the bowl rest in my lap. Talon is eating methodically, the bottom of the mask pulled up with one hand, so he can shove the fork into his mouth with the other. I let my hair fall around my face, so I can watch him surreptitiously. He wears a gray short-sleeved T-shirt, so his arms are visible. At the top of one arm, just peeking out from under the fabric of his shirt, is the white bandage covering the stab wound I gave him. He looks vulnerable compared to the others.

Scar is hunched in a corner, his back to us. He slurps and belches his way through his meal, the mask pushed way back on his head. He finishes eating just as a news broadcaster announces the day's headlines. I am surprised that I am being allowed to watch this. Denying prisoners any knowledge of the outside world is a well-known way of making them co-operate. But then, I have already cooperated—maybe they are preparing to send me home? Maybe the government has agreed with Dad that releasing Kyle Jefferies is a small price to pay for my freedom.

"We go live now to a press conference with Prime Minister Stephen Knollys-Green," the anchorwoman says.

And there he is. My dad, in his yellow tie—the one I picked out for him on that last morning—standing behind a podium on the steps of Downing Street with my mum a step behind him. The camera zooms in on Dad as he loops his arm around Mum and pulls her into the frame. She is thin, her eyes watery behind the TV makeup. I can sense her resistance to being that close to him on camera from the puckering of her lips and the way she tilts her head back. Dad begins to talk, but his voice is quiet, and his hand shakes as he reaches for the glass of water on the podium. That makes me nervous. I need him to be in charge. To be terrifying. I need him to tell these people that they can't hurt his daughter and he will do whatever it takes to get me back. Instead he talks slowly, tripping over his words, and his eyes flutter across the screen as if unable to focus properly. "Firstly, I—we—would like to . . . thank everyone for their unfailing support in the form of words of condolence, letters, e-mails, and even gifts. These acts of kindness have sustained us through these, our darkest of days."

I convince myself he is just taking time to warm up. I've seen Dad persuade the United Nations to send out peace-keeping troops. He can do this.

"These last days have been . . . They have been . . . well, hell. As many of you know, on the eleventh of April, my daughter Robyn was taken hostage while traveling with her mother and sister—"

He gets no further because my mum collapses, falling right into the podium and knocking it forward. My hand goes automatically to my head as hers hits the concrete. She doesn't get up again. The room spins. I stare at a piece of peeling wallpaper, just to the right of the screen. Green with mold and curved upward, it looks like a leaf. I stare at it until the room settles. *Be okay. Please be okay.* I jump as Talon touches my arm. When I look at him, I expect to see gloating in his eyes, but there is only gentleness there, as if he cares whether my mum might be hurt. I've never thought before how much you can tell about a person from just their eyes. When I look back at the TV screen, my heartbeat is steadier again. Like somehow the fact that I'm not the only one in this room who cares about my mum has calmed me. One of Dad's assistants is helping Mum to her feet. She looks dazed but otherwise all right.

"Stupid bitch," Scar murmurs.

Talon tells him to shut up. Scar opens his mouth to say something but is silenced by Feather holding up her hand. "He's going to start talking again."

She's right. Dad is back at the podium. Talon's hand slips from my arm, but my skin is still warm from his touch. After a last look at Mum, who is being ushered inside Number 10, Dad begins to talk. It's like he's a different man. Maybe seeing Mum faint has reminded him of what is at stake. There is a new determination set into the lines in his face, and he grips the sides of the podium with both hands, like he might throw it at anyone who gets in his way. When he speaks, it is the voice he used for the UN. This is the dad I need him to be right now. He is, after all, fighting for my life.

"As many of you know, on the eleventh of April, my sixteen-year-old daughter, my Robyn, was kidnapped while traveling with her mother and sister to my wife's family home in the country by the terrorist organization the AFC. This same group is responsible for shooting me in Paris in January. These people are ruthless. They would have us believe that they are promoting the rights of animals, but what about the rights of the human? What about the rights of my daughter, snatched in the most brutal and terrifying way? This will not be tolerated. We will find the people responsible and we will punish them in the severest way." He looks straight into the camera, straight at me. "Robyn, we will find you. We will bring you home."

A flush of adrenaline surges through me. I knew Dad would sort this. Everything is going to be okay.

"Terrorists seek to destroy the fabric of our society and put in its place chaos, destruction, and fear," Dad continues. "They will stop at nothing until their ends are met. The fact that they believe that taking children hostage is a viable way to promote their cause is testimony to this."

"This is utter bullshit," Scar says. He leans over the back of the sofa; his bowl lies discarded on the table, pasta sauce crusting on its edges. "Your father is full of shit, you know that, Princess?" His fingers slide under my hair and up the back of my neck.

I jerk forward.

"Scar, sit down over there," Feather orders.

Dad is still talking. He mentions the video I made in which I demanded the release of Kyle Jefferies. He brands Jefferies a terrorist. In fact, he is talking a lot about terrorism and how it must be stamped out. "We must work together to ensure the safety of this entire nation." He holds his hands out, palms up. It is a gesture he often uses. It is supposed to be nonthreatening and to invite friendship and cooperation. I was in the room when the speechwriter first suggested it. All my dad's speeches are written for him, carefully and elaborately scripted by a team of people. He oversees them and makes suggestions, of course, but he doesn't write them. He wrote this one, though, didn't he? He wouldn't let someone else write the speech that could save his daughter's life. Would he?

"Terrorism cannot and will not be tolerated." He bangs his hand firmly on the podium, and for a moment, the speech feels like a performance. Almost as though Dad is going through the motions. But for who? For the cameras? The AFC. For *me*. Why go on camera at all, looking cleanly shaven and neat in his suit and tie, like his daughter being kidnapped is a press opportunity to prove that he is a good man in a crisis? He doesn't look at all like a man whose daughter has been kidnapped. He looks like a prime minister, using an opportunity to talk about terrorism.

Stop it, Robyn. Stop it. He's the prime minister. Of course he needs to be in control. I need him to be in control; that's what will bring me home. But why hasn't he just given the AFC what they want? Release Marble and this will all be over. In a few hours I could be back at Downing Street, with

Mum and Addy and Shadow. Any second now he'll say it.

Instead he says, "I want to say this to the people who are holding my daughter: Let Robyn go. Give yourselves up. This is not the way to get what you want. I will not be bribed, cajoled, or bullied. This is a futile mission. Let her go now and we will be lenient." His right arm on the podium, he stares deep into the camera. It is another of his "moves" and is designed to make viewers feel like he is speaking directly to them. And right now, he is speaking directly to me and saying that he will do anything but the one thing that will secure my release.

Dad's speech is finished. His press secretary opens the floor to questions. I can't believe it. Why hasn't he agreed to the terms? The words *This is a futile mission* roll around in my mind.

One reporter shouts out, "In the video the AFC posted online, Robyn demanded the immediate release of Kyle Jefferies. Will you be doing that?"

"I want to make it absolutely clear that we are doing everything we can to bring Robyn home," Dad says.

"And that includes allowing a known terrorist back onto our streets?"

"I didn't say that." Dad falters. He takes a sip from his glass of water—something he's been taught to do when he needs to think about his answer. It's a stalling tactic. But why does he need to think about this answer? Of course he is going to release Marble. He has said he will do anything to bring me home. Dad replaces the glass on the podium. His hand trembles as he does so. "I want to make it clear that Robyn's safety is our first priority. We are in contact with the AFC, and we are working through a plan to bring her home. But Britain has not been, nor will it ever be, bullied or blackmailed by terrorists. These people will release my daughter, or they will face the severest consequences."

The other journalists all ask variations of the same question. After a while the press secretary intervenes, ushering my dad back inside. The door to Number 10 shuts behind him. I feel numb as Feather switches the TV off.

Scar says what we are all thinking: "Looks like somebody's not daddy's little princess after all."

CHAPTER EIGHT

My mum cried on the afternoon of the election results. It was shortly before the car came to collect us and take us to our new home at Number 10. She'd gone upstairs to put on her face. It's always a big photo opportunity, and the advisers had picked out an outfit for Mum especially. I'd followed her up to her room. Dad wasn't back from Buckingham Palace and the house felt oddly empty, as though we'd already left it. As I walked into the master bedroom, Mum sat frozen at her vanity table, one hand on her enormous belly. My baby sister was due in four months. I could see that Mum had been crying. She picked up her hairbrush when she saw me, like she wanted to hide the fact that she'd been sitting, staring at nothing.

"Are you okay?" I asked.

"Of course." She waved me away with the brush. "Hurry up and get dressed. The entire nation won't want to be kept waiting by you."

I didn't leave. Instead I sat down on the bed, next to the

neat blue twinset that had been laid out on it, and fingered the pearl button on one of the cuffs. "Everything's going to be different now, isn't it?"

She didn't answer. She was rubbing her stomach.

"Is she kicking?"

Mum smiled. "Your new sister is going to be an acrobat. Come here. Come and see."

I crouched down beside her and put my hand on her tummy. "Ha. There. That's brilliant."

Mum stroked my hair off my face. "Your fringe is always in your eyes. It's a shame. You've got such pretty eyes."

"I have Dad's eyes."

Her mouth pinched. "Yes," she said. "Yes, you do." She stroked my hair absently for a while longer. Normally I would have pulled away, but I was scared that day. I knew there would be loads of cameras waiting for us on the ride to Downing Street, and I already felt homesick. Mum said I could decorate the new room however I wanted. It didn't matter; it still wouldn't be home. "Your father's a good man deep down," she said as if she were answering a question. "He loves you very much. No matter what happens, I want you to remember that."

"Are you getting divorced or something?" The parents of a couple of girls at school had split up. I didn't want that to happen. Also, it seemed like really bad timing, as Dad had just been made PM.

Mum must have thought the same thing, because she laughed. "That would not fit with your father's election promises. This is going to be a big change for all of us, but for your father most of all. He will be in charge of a whole country now. An enormous privilege and a great responsibility. You—we—will come first in his heart, of course, but sometimes your dad may have to make choices . . . difficult ones . . . that we may not agree with or understand. He may not always be able to explain them to us."

I hadn't known until this moment what Mum had meant or why it had made her sad. Dad had squirmed on camera because he was lying when he said they would do anything to bring me home. All he has to do is release Kyle Jefferies; it's that simple. Surely the police could just recapture him again as soon as I'm safe?

But a part of me knows it is not that easy. How can the British government be seen negotiating terms with kidnappers? It would make Britain seem vulnerable. If I'm being honest, I have half-known this all along. I just didn't want to believe it. I was sure Dad would find a way to bend the rules. This is me. His daughter. Despite Mum's warning on election day, I always believed that no matter what, I would be his priority. Before politics. Before his job. Before his ambition. Even though he has missed parents' evenings and my GCSE art show and Addy's third birthday and my twelfth and fourteenth—when it mattered, I was sure that he would stop being the PM for as long as was needed, and he would just be Dad.

The patches of light and dark on the wooden floor of the living room form patterns like waves on a beach. I feel like I am sinking into that sand. Everything I knew about my dad and his beliefs—the absolute faith I have placed in him to do the right thing—is falling away. I feel unsteady in this new world. More is at stake now, though, than my relationship with my dad. If Feather doubts, like I do, the sincerity of Dad's promise to do everything he can to bring me home, then my life is worth nothing to her and she will kill me.

Feather is furiously pacing the room, her nostrils flaring. "He is making idiots of us." Scar flicks manically between news channels, hoping for updates, until Feather seizes the remote control and flings it across the room. It lands between me and Talon. He has not moved since the news broadcast, but he sits forward now to place the TV remote on the table. His expression is hard to read. If I had to guess, I'd say he is feeling sorry for me, like somehow he knows what watching my dad abandon me on national TV feels like. Which is ridiculous. And yet, despite kidnapping me, I sense that he is a good person. I wonder, not for the first time, what brought him here.

Talon snatches at Feather's hand as she passes, pulling her to a stop. "We need to stay calm," he says, looping his fingers with hers.

"How can I be calm?" she asks. "When my brother is locked up and they are doing God knows what to him! Robyn, it seems your little video wasn't convincing enough."

"She wasn't scared enough," Scar says.

"Hmm," Feather responds. "But maybe her father will be more willing to cooperate if *both* of his daughters have been taken hostage."

I leap up from the sofa. "No! You can't take Addy. Please. She hasn't done anything. She's tiny. She's only a baby. *Please!*" I say.

Talon's voice cuts into my rising hysteria. "It wouldn't work anyway. We'd never get close enough again. Security will have been stepped up like crazy. It's a miracle we managed it this time. Fee, we need to think things through. Stay calm."

"Will you stop telling me to be calm? It is really pissing me off." Feather goes over to Scar. "What do you think we should do?"

"Kill her."

You have no idea how you are going to react in certain situations until you're in them. Until Scar said those words, I'd never really thought about what it meant to die, to no longer exist. I'm sixteen years old. I can't die. Why didn't Dad just give up Kyle? *Oh God, I can't die here. Not like this.*

It is Talon who speaks next. His voice is steady, a thrumming muscle in his neck the only evidence of how tense he really is. "It's kind of hard to bargain with a dead body."

He is arguing for me to live. Why? I don't know, but it gives me a second to think. "What has the negotiator promised you?" I ask.

"Shut up," Scar says. "Who said you could speak?"

"What are you talking about, Princess?" Feather asks, ignoring him.

"The person you are talking to about Kyle. The contact between you and my dad." My brain is turning over, fast. There must be a negotiator.

Feather nods. *Go on.*

"He is the one who'll be able to arrange stuff. Dad . . . Dad can't admit to any secret talks on TV. That press conference would have been just for the cameras."

Is that true? Could it really have been a performance, not for me, not for the AFC, but for the rest of the world? Suddenly it feels like a possibility. A dangerous, stupid possibility, but one all the same. Of course Dad can't be seen to be cooperating with terrorists. But a negotiator could promise anything in private. The thought gives me new confidence. "The negotiator is probably getting ready to free Kyle right now. If . . . if you"—*don't say kill*—"hurt me, they won't let you have your brother."

"I'm aware of how an exchange works, Princess," Feather says coldly.

"She's talking crap. What does she know about this stuff?" Scar says.

"She's his daughter. She knows him." Feather pauses, then says, "We wait. We kill her and we've got nothing left to bargain with. She lives, for now."

Next to me, Talon sighs. In relief? Is that possible? The important thing now is that Dad is coming for me. He is doing everything he can to save me. He just can't tell anyone about it. I ignore the small doubt inside me. It is going to be okay. I *am* going home.

There is some more discussion between Scar and Feather, but Feather wins, as usual. She tells Scar, "Take her back to her cell. I'm sick of looking at her."

Scar cracks his knuckles, but Talon stands up. "I'll do it."

"I want to talk to you," Feather says.

"We can talk later. You said we needed the girl."

"I'm not going to kill her," Scar says with a feral grin.

Talon ignores him and draws Feather to one side. He's dropped his voice, but I pick up the odd word: "Unstable . . . Need her. Safe."

"Fine," Feather says finally, "you take her back downstairs." She turns to me. "We are going to make another home movie soon, Princess, and you'd better hope they release my brother. Otherwise . . ." She draws one finger slowly across her throat.

• • •

Feather says we will make the new film today. It is only my fifth day here, but time passes so slowly in this cell that one minute feels like three weeks. At times it is as if I have been here forever. All the things that came before belong to some other Robyn.

I am flicking through the book Talon gave me, because it is better than staring at the walls, imagining how my kidnappers might kill me if Dad doesn't give them what they want. I have been trying to think positively. To conjure up images of secret agents crashing through my window and knocking Feather out with a swift roundhouse kick to the head before leading me to safety. Those thoughts are as delicate as smoke, though, and evaporate immediately. It is the visions of Feather pointing a gun at my chest that solidify inside my mind.

I turn a page of the book. I don't much care about birds, but the photographs are beautiful. I get a lump in my throat just looking at them. One of my favorites is of a bird with iridescent blue tail feathers, pecking at a red berry. I wish I could take photos like that. The description on the opposite page tells me it is a jay. "A colorful crow, about the same size as a jackdaw. Jays are sociable birds with the ability to mimic others' songs. When out bird-watching, listen for a *krar krar*—this is their alarm call." I turn the page. My namesake, a robin, its red chest puffed up, perches on a snowy branch. "Britain's national bird. Their sweet song—*twiddle-oo twiddle-eedee*—often leads them to be mistaken for nightingales."

I glance over a few more pages, but I can't identify the birds outside, and really, who cares? I push the book off my lap more forcefully than I mean to. It lands facedown on the floor. When I pick it up, I notice that the jay's page is torn and crumpled. I flatten it out and then close the book, feeling sad. I've managed to ruin the one beautiful thing in this place.

The door opens, and I push the book under the pillow. I don't want Talon to know a page is ripped.

Feather stands in the doorway, a pair of scissors clutched in her hand.

She gives no explanation as she drags me from the cell and down the hall, into the bathroom. She doesn't even bother to cover my eyes. She shoves me forward now, and I stumble into the bathtub. "What—what are you going to do?" I ask.

"Just a little trim." She snaps the scissors at me.

"Of what?"

"Your hair, stupid."

I snatch my hair up into a ponytail at the back my neck. As I do so, I catch a whiff of Mum's shampoo, which I used to wash it on the day I was taken. The smell must be in my head; my hair stinks of grease and sweat. But I don't want Feather to cut it. I wonder if this has anything to do with

Talon standing up for me. It's a fleeting thought, not full-formed, and it vanishes the second that Feather moves toward me with the scissors. Then my whole attention is focused on keeping her at bay and keeping hold of my hair.

She lunges and I duck, but not quickly enough, and the blade opens a thin cut down my arm. I don't want to let go of my hair, so I only have one arm to defend myself. Feather may be tiny, but she is strong. It quickly becomes clear that I'm no match for her. She tugs on my forearm, her skinny fingers digging into the graze and making my eyes sting. She forces me to sit on the edge of the tub, and she jabs the point of the scissors into the hand holding my hair until I let go. Then she wrenches my head back.

A moment later, I hear a *snip* and feel a tug on my scalp. My hair falls to the floor in a ribbon.

"Why?" I whimper.

"To show we're serious." Feather stands up and puts the scissors in her pocket.

Long dark strands of my hair lie scattered across the bathroom floor. I grab a handful of it and try to stand. I have to use the sink to steady myself. It's like I've been beaten. Hands trembling, I touch my head, so gently, like it is a wound. I can't bring myself to look in the mirror. I duck my head automatically, but there's no curtain of hair to protect me. The hair in my hand is soft and I loop it around my fingers. I never realized before how much my hair was a part of who I am.

Feather smiles at me. "You look like a soldier now. You look ready for the revolution."

My cell is a TV studio again, only this time it is not Scar operating the camera. A small remote in Feather's hand does that. Oh, and this time I won't be talking. My mouth is gagged and I am bound to a wooden chair. The lamp is also back, and it's pointed right into my eyes. Every time I turn my head out of its glare, Feather pushes me back into it. She could have tugged me by my hair, but there isn't enough of it left now. Not after she hacked it off this morning. That scene in the bathroom keeps playing over and over in my mind. Every time Feather moves too quickly, I flinch.

Feather has been talking for what feels like hours. A muscle over her upper lip is ticking rhythmically, like the countdown to something. She is angry. Her voice is as powerful as a river in full flood. I think of something Dad once told me, what some previous PM had said about a fanatic being someone who can't change their mind and won't change the subject. Feather talks about corporate greed and the devastating effect humans are having on the planet. She talks about social injustice and surveillance and corruption and complicity and revenge. She talks about illegal drug testing, not just on animals but sometimes on humans, too, in poorer countries where people turn to trials in a desperate attempt to get themselves and their families the drugs they need or even just to earn some extra money. She talks about a million other things too, but I am losing focus. A lock of my severed hair is still wrapped around my fingers, and I keep stroking it over and over. In my mind, I am at home on my bed with Shadow. *Stroke, Kitty. Stroke, Kitty.* My brain is foggy. It won't cooperate like it usually does. That scares me. I can't fall apart. I am all that I have in here.

Feather goes on and on. "You seek to demonize us by labeling us as terrorists because we are threatening your status quo—your world of inherited wealth and privilege. We are not the enemy of the people, though. We are their salvation. A revolution is coming, Mr. Prime Minister. We will live together in harmony on a planet that we seek to care for and sustain, without harming any of its creatures or resources in the pursuit of our own ends." Feather shakes me by the neck like a dog. "Do not make your own daughter the first sacrifice in the coming war. Give me back my brother. Save your daughter's life." From her pocket, Feather pulls out something shiny: a strip of silver in the lamplight.

A knife.

Oh my God.

I shriek into the gag as she slices one of my wrists free from the bindings that were holding it to the chair. Her fingers dig into my skin, and she doesn't let go, no matter how much I struggle. "And if you don't cooperate," she snarls at the camera, "I will send your daughter back in pieces. You can have the first piece now; let's call it a show of good faith." And as the knife rips into my index finger, I open my mouth and scream.

CHAPTER NINE

It is the sound of Feather's voice that brings me around. "I'm not a monster, you know. Whatever you think." My eyelids slide open just enough to see Talon standing in the middle of my room and Feather slumping against the wall, looking as tiny and frail as a bird. Neither of them is looking my way. My arm is at my side. I don't want to look too closely at my hand. It hurts like hell. The bedsheets must be slick with blood. I can't imagine how ugly the wound will be. Thankfully, I must have passed out before Feather really began hacking at it. Through bone. Oh. My stomach turns over, and the small slice of world I can see spins. I close my eyes again.

Feather is speaking. "I just want my brother back. Surely, you of all people can understand that."

"We shouldn't be hurting her. It won't help our cause."

"You still care about that then?"

"How dare you ask me that! Jez was my brother. Marble is my friend. This is just all so messed up. Why did you have to cut her? And what did you do to her hair?"

"She needed a trim."

"There is something *wrong* with you."

Feather laughs. "You heard that prick on TV. We're doing everything we can, blah, pissing blah. Well, I'm in charge here, not them, and I say they aren't doing enough. They needed a short, sharp shock, and they got one."

"This is not what I signed up for. You can't abuse her like this. It's disgusting. And immoral!"

"You have the prime minister's daughter tied up in the basement, and you want to talk to me about morality? Get a grip, Talon. You are doing what you need to do. For your brother. For my brother. Or have you forgotten about them?"

"None of that is her fault."

"Robyn and her dad aren't so different. They are part of the same elite. The governing force. She doesn't care about us."

"You don't know her."

"And you do? Damn it, Talon. This is about more than just your brother. This is about changing the status quo. We are fighting back. Come on! Look at us. Look at what we can achieve. First we get Marble back, and then it's all going to change. Everything. Him being released will be one almighty finger up to the establishment."

"But Jez will still be dead."

Even with my eyes closed, I can sense the tension between them. There's a long silence, broken only by a single tweet from outside, a sweet *twiddle-oo twiddle-eedee*.

"I want Marble back as much as you do, but what we're doing here scares me. It's too much," Talon says.

"Everything scares you," she snaps, but there's something like disappointment in her voice. When she speaks next, it's gone, and her tone is efficient and cold, like an elastic band snapping back into place. "Don't forget who's in charge here. You're in too deep now to back out. Trust me. I know what I'm doing. This is just the beginning. We'll get revenge for Jez. We'll get revenge for everything."

Talon cuts in. "Maybe we shouldn't be talking like this here. She could wake up."

"I don't care if she does. A new world is coming, and you and I are going to be right at the heart of it. Those politicians, bankers, and corporate arseholes won't know what's hit them. Just look at her. She's so stupid! No thought in the world that Daddy dearest isn't perfect. Makes me want to cut off all her fingers . . . Don't look at me like that. I'm not going to do it. But she makes me so angry. She lives in the seat of power and she doesn't give a shit about anything. She doesn't ask real questions. Just, 'What dress shall I wear to this party?' I hate people like her. The ignorance. The sense of entitlement."

"He's her dad; she trusts him."

"Well, he's a lying son of a bitch, and we are going to expose him."

"We still shouldn't hurt her anymore. She's scared."

"She's the hostage! Of course she's scared. What did you expect? But all right . . . all right . . . we won't hurt her anymore. Maybe get her a blanket and a teddy bear? Read her a bedtime story?"

"Don't be like this. This isn't you."

"This is me! This is exactly who I have always been, Talon. It's you who's changed. Now, get a grip. I need you to stop being a pussy and help me get my brother back."

I am alone a long while before I muster up the courage to look at my hand. The bandage is so crusted with blood that it's no longer white but a dirty brown. But that isn't what surprises me. I peel off the piece of sticky tape holding the wrappings in place and then slowly unravel the gauze. . . . The cut beneath is ugly and deep, but it is just that: a cut. My index finger remains intact, and more amazingly, it is still attached to my left hand. I wiggle it. The wound smarts and bleeds again, but the finger moves easily. I lost consciousness very shortly after she had begun cutting me. I just assumed she had gone through with it. Why didn't she? Why pretend?

I'm not a monster. Whatever you think.

I realize that it is enough for Dad to *think* that she's cut my finger off. She didn't actually need to do it. And that gives me hope. She could have killed me any number of times, or beaten me, or let Scar attack me, but she hasn't. She's shouted at me and hurt me, but she's never totally lost control. Never done any irreparable damage. Maybe, just maybe, I will survive this.

I flex my finger again, relishing the pain now because it means I still have feeling in it. I still have ten fingers.

Talon takes me to the bathroom. It is the first time I've been out of my cell since Feather cut my hair off. I feel awkward; I keep lowering my chin, expecting my hair to fall around my face like it used to, but of course there isn't enough of it anymore. And I can't stop tugging on it, as if that will somehow make it grow. The clump I took from the floor is in my pocket, and I slip my hand inside to hold it.

When we reach the bathroom, Talon tells me not to be too long, but it's habit now. He lets me take as long as I like. I go inside and stand by the door, looking at the floor. I need to pee, but first I have to see my hair. I'm not brave enough to look yet. It is ten counts before I take my first step, another ten before the second, and a good fifty before I finally manage to force myself to gaze at the mirror.

My hair hangs in dirty tangles down to my ears; it's shorter in some places and longer in others, but all shorter than my fringe used to be. Without hair framing it, my wide face stretches endlessly, rising to the crest of my nose and then sloping into the dip in my chin. My eyes are larger too: vast, muddy pools in a desert of face and scalp.

Who am I now? Is it really so easy to wipe out a

personality? Will this new person that I've become still fight with everything she has just to survive one more day, one more minute? Will she hold on even after every tiny shred of hope is gone? Will she protect her little sister with her dying breath if she has to?

The girl in the mirror blinks. She looks tired and lonely and scared. She doesn't feel like me at all.

I tuck a strand behind my ear, like my mum did on that last day. It immediately falls forward into my eyes again. There's no trace left of Mum's shampoo. I want my mum. I want her to tell me that it's okay, it'll grow back. I want her to laugh and say she never liked my fringe anyway. But she isn't here. There's no one here but me. I want to go home.

A lump rises in my throat. I try to bite back the tears, but this time a few escape, and that makes more come because, out of everything I've endured, it is losing my hair that has finally broken me. Am I the stuck-up princess Feather says I am? I never asked my dad enough about his work. Maybe if I had, I wouldn't be here now, waiting and hoping for a rescue party that is never going to come.

There's a knock on the door.

"Go away!" I shout.

"Robyn, please, let me in."

There's a calmness in Talon's voice that something inside me yearns for, and before I've even registered what I'm doing, I've opened the door. Talon stands on the threshold, his eyes dark with pity. And that makes me mad, because I don't want him to feel sorry for me. I want him to let me go. RIGHT NOW.

I scream at him, but even as I do, I know that it's not about him. I'm screaming at this stupid bathroom, at my own vanity for caring about my stupid, stupid, stupid hair and most of all at my dad, because I need him now and he's not here. Why hasn't he come for me? Why has he left me here like this, alone? The scream is loud and angry and filled with all the pain I will ever feel in my entire life, because nothing can ever be as bad as this. And just for a little while I want someone else to pick up the pieces of who I used to be and to put them together again, because I can't remember how.

Talon flinches, but he lets me yell right in his face. I shout until there's nothing left inside me, only a calmness as still and empty as my prison cell. Then I drop back, falling against the sink, like all my energy has left with my yelling. Only then does Talon come forward into the bathroom. He moves very slowly, as though around a caged tiger, to sit on the bathtub. I stay resting against the sink, its edges making grooves in the palms of my hands. Neither of us speaks. Neither of us moves for a long time.

Finally Talon says, "Robins are very resilient birds, you know, and incredibly territorial. They will do anything to protect their families. They've even been known to fight with much bigger birds, if necessary."

"And who usually wins?" I wipe my cheek with the back of my hand, but most of my tears have already dried up. "Actually, don't answer that."

"Feather will let you go, when your father gives her what she wants."

"And if he doesn't?"

Talon says nothing, because there's nothing to say.

My legs hurt from standing and the floor is grubby, so I drop down next to him on the edge of the bath. It's a tiny space, and our arms almost touch. I remember how warm his hand felt on my skin in the living room, and I let my arm fall against his. He looks up. There's an intensity in his eyes, like he just wants me to understand that he's actually a good person. It scares me suddenly how much I want to believe that. I look away, up at the tiny grating. "What's it like out there today? The weather, I mean."

"Gray. Miserable."

Tears rise up again, so I shut my eyes and imagine a charcoal sky, fading to tarnished silver on the horizon. It is magnificent. It is the same sky that hangs over Addy and my mum and my dad. I want to be standing under that sky. I want to feel the lick of wind on my face. I want the rain to kiss my cheeks. And I want to see all the birds I don't have names for. I miss my family.

I don't realize I've said it out loud, until Talon says, "Me too."

"Your brother's dead?"

"Yes, and my dad."

The silence between us stretches from here to Canada.

"I'm sorry."

"Why?"

"I don't know. It's just what people say."

"Why did you go into politics?" I ask Dad. We are walking back toward the hotel along the Seine. Dad's meeting with the French president isn't until Thursday, and that means we still have a whole day, just the two of us. Well, five of us, if you include Gordon, Harold, and Mary (Dad's secretary), none of whom are ever far away. For the moment, though, it is just Dad and me and the river. Gordon is hanging back, talking on his mobile. It's late afternoon, and the winter sunlight is thin. It will be dark soon, and the shadows of the buildings hang long over the cobbled banks.

"I wanted to do good," Dad says.

I blow a raspberry. "Cliché alert. Try again."

"I wanted to protect people. Build a better world for our children."

I blow two raspberries. "Are you trying to make me throw up? Come on, old man. Tell the truth for once in your life. You're a politician, so I know that's hard for you, but come on!"

"The truth; there is no truth."

"Is this one of those 'There is no tree' things?"

Dad isn't listening to my bad existentialism, though. He is staring across the river. 'Truth is a fabrication. There is never only one truth. Only versions of it." Dad nods at the bridge ahead of us. "Le Pont de l'Archevêché. The lovers' bridge. Couples attach engraved padlocks to the railings and then throw the keys into the river."

"Do you and Mum have one?"

"Yes."

"You should have made it a combination lock."

Dad looks at me sadly. "Robyn, you know your mother and I—"

But I walk on ahead of him. "Can we go and see the padlocks?" I don't want another "Your mother and I love you and Adriana very much" or "All marriages have their difficulties" conversation. I have heard it before too many times.

As we approach the base of the bridge, Dad says suddenly, "I meant what I said about going into politics to help people. To make a difference. To do good."

"And have you?" The daylight is almost gone now. My dad is standing a step in front of me—a dark silhouette against a fading sky. Behind him, the thousands of padlocks chained to the bridge wink in the last glow of the sun. "Dad?"

"Yes . . . yes. On balance, I believe I have done more good than bad."

I laugh then and slide my arm through his. "You could never do anything bad."

"I hope you always believe that, Bobs."

"I will," I say, just as all the streetlights in Paris flick on and the river is filled with streamers of green and blue and gold.

"Enjoying the book?" Talon asks the next afternoon, while returning me to my cell after a trip to the bathroom. There are now six scratches on the wall under my bed.

"The photos are nice." It's only been a day since I screamed at him, but already there's been a shift between us. I've begun looking up expectantly whenever the key has turned in the lock. I'm noticing little things about him too, like how there is a tiny fleck of brown in his right iris, or how his walk is ever so slightly lopsided, or how I can tell he's smiling by the creases at the corners of his eyes.

He was surprisingly calm about the torn page in his book. I told him this morning when he brought my breakfast. "Accidents happen," was all he said. Now I point at a photo of a dark-brown bird that I've wanted to show him for a while. "This one is great. It reminds me of one I saw at the wildlife photography exhibition last year. It's not the same bird. The one I saw was green, bright green, with an orange beak and a tufty darker green patch on top, like a cowlick."

"Was it a parrot?" he asks.

"No. I don't know what it was, and I know what a parrot

124

looks like. Anyway, it's not about what type of bird it was. Just that it was looking at you, head cocked, like it was assessing you. In this photo, the bird—"

"A crossbill."

"—is doing the same thing. How come you know so much about this stuff?"

He sits down next to me on the bed. "Just picked it up over the years. My dad was into bird-watching. He wanted me and my brother to get into it too. I thought it was lame at first."

"But you changed your mind?"

He shrugs. "Jez got really sick, and suddenly doing things as a family meant more. We'd always go out bird-watching on the days when Jez was well enough."

"Was it fun?"

"No, it's as boring as you'd expect. It's cold, and nothing happens for hours. Sometimes you can go the whole time without seeing anything, but when you do, it's amazing. And you get kind of addicted to that rush. I saw a white-tailed eagle once." He catches my blank look. "They are seriously rare. Even went extinct for a while and had to be reintroduced into the wild. They have these huge wings with what look like fingers on the ends. They are stunning. Seeing something like that makes all the waiting about in the cold worth it."

"Photography's like that," I say. "Waiting ages in the freezing cold for one photo. And if you're me, it isn't even that good. Not like these." I turn the pages of the book, stopping at a picture of a ball of beige downy feathers and two enormous dark eyes. "Oh, he is cute."

"That's Bert."

"You named the pictures in your book?"

"I didn't. My brother, Jez, did."

It's the kind of thing Addy would do, only she'd want to call him Princess something or other. She'd slap her hand on the page and say, "Stroke owl, Byn. Stroke, stroke."

"You must miss him," I say.

"Yeah. He didn't deserve what happened to him. None of us did." Talon sounds angry.

I shouldn't care about Talon's brother, but I do. Last night I even found myself thinking about what Talon's face is like. His eyes are special. Is it weird to wonder if the rest of him is?

I ask him what the weather is like outside. It's beginning to feel like a thing between us, and for some reason that matters to me.

Talon's answer is gruff this time. "Dunno. Sunny, maybe. I haven't been outside."

He leaves shortly after. Last night after dinner and then again this morning, he apologized for locking me in, but today he goes silently. It feels as though I've done something wrong.

• • •

It is late evening on the seventh day. How can I have only been here for a week? It seems like a lifetime. We read a book at school by a guy who had been held hostage for fourteen years. He kept himself sane and fit by sticking to a routine. A set number of laps of his cell each day. A set number of push-ups. When he became weaker, or was tied up, he would do smaller exercises and imagine doing the larger ones. I can't think about being locked up here for fourteen years. No amount of exercising would keep me sane. I get up off the bed and begin to walk around the room. It can't hurt to keep fit. After four laps, I cross the room in three big strides and then take five normal paces back. The next time across, I make nine really tiny steps.

It is nine shuffles, two and a half side steps, and one somersault—just—between the edge of the bed and the door. I pirouette, skip, jog backward and forward, walk like a bear, stride like a tiger, tiptoe like a mouse, and swing one arm like an elephant's trunk.

After a while, I begin to pace the room again, moving faster and faster, concentrating on the pounding in my chest, the pull of my muscles, and the slap of my Converses against the tiled floor and trying to push all other thoughts away.

When I'm on my fourteenth lap, the door opens. I look up, expecting Talon. But instead Scar is standing in the doorway, his mouth screwed up into a warped grin.

"Hello, Princess," he says.

CHAPTER TEN

In the instant before he grabs me, I see that Scar's eyes are red in the glare of the bare bulb. I can't move quickly enough and he pushes me against the wall, his hands on my shoulders. He's so close I can't help but take in the stench of him—the stale alcohol combined with rot, like something has crawled inside him to die. I squirm, but he holds me fast. My feeble punches to his ribs have no effect either. "Gentle there, Princess. You don't want to break a nail. No need to be afraid. I just want a little chat. We never get any time together, just you and me."

Panic is rising inside of me like a tidal wave until I remember the knife in his belt. Will it still be there? He is telling me that we should be friends. "Maybe I could help you."

"How?" I ask, feeling for the handle of the knife through his T-shirt. "Will you let me go?" My fumbling fingers lift the fabric very, very gently.

"Let you go? Well, I don't know about that, but maybe I could be persuaded."

My hand closes around the knife. I pull it free.

"Oi, what are you doing?"

I jab the blade into his side—the fleshy bit just above the waistband of his trousers.

His hands go instinctively to his injury. I make a dash for the door, tugging desperately on the handle, but it is locked.

"You'll pay for that," he says. I turn to see him tug the knife out easily. And I realize how stupid I have been. The door is locked, and he is stronger. All I have done is remind him that he has a knife.

"Help! Somebody, please!" I scream as I bang my fists against the door.

Scar drags me backward by what is left of my hair. "HELP ME!" I scream.

There's the sound of feet pounding down the stairs to the basement, then along the hall. The door is flung open, and there's Talon. I've never been so happy to see someone.

"Get away from her," Talon growls.

"What you going to do about it?" Scar tightens his grip on the blade.

"Robyn, come here. We're going upstairs."

Scar is blocking my path to the doorway. "Piss off, Talon."

"No. Move out of the way and let Robyn go."

"You want a fight? That it? Well, come on then. Show me what you've got."

Scar is talking to Talon, but it is me who makes a move.

I run at Scar, knocking him off balance, but not enough. He shoves me backward, and I fall onto the bed. Talon comes at him from the other side. Scar brushes him off easily, then jabs at his face with the knife, tearing his mask. Blood drips down Talon's chin. Scar lunges again, this time aiming for Talon's belly. At the last second, Talon moves out of the way and seizes Scar by the wrist, propelling him around before slamming him against the wall. Talon shoves his forearm into Scar's throat and uses his free hand to ram Scar's into the plaster again and again until the knife clatters to the floor. Talon kicks it away. Scar is strong and crafty, though. He punches Talon in the head with his now-free hand. Talon reels backward from the blow and Scar pounces, pushing Talon onto the floor and crouching over him, both hands around his throat.

Neither of them is taking any notice of me. The door to my cell is open and unguarded. I could run so easily. I look at the door; I look at Talon. He is gasping for breath, eyes bulging. He saved me. I can't leave him here to die.

The discarded knife is by Scar's ankle. Before I change my mind, I pick it up and hold it shakily to Scar's throat. "Let him go." I press the blade into his skin, and a trickle of blood runs down his neck. "Let go of Talon and then stand up slowly."

"You haven't got the guts," Scar sneers.

I press the blade even harder against his throat, until a

stream of blood flows freely. "I've done it before."

He releases Talon, who immediately rolls over, coughing and spluttering. I glance down at him for only a second, but it's enough time for Scar to clamp a hand around my wrist. I cry out and drop the knife. Scar stands up, catching both of my hands in one of his, and then shoves me backward until the edge of the bed takes my legs out from underneath me.

He growls at me. It turns into a wince as he stoops to pick up the knife. His hand goes automatically first to his side and then to the gash at his throat. Blood is dripping from both, and he is clearly in pain. He seems to hesitate, his eyes assessing me and Talon. Then he secures his grip on the blade and takes a step closer to Talon. I gasp as the blade flashes down in a clean arc to sink deep into the floor, millimeters from Talon's head.

"You deserve each other," Scar says as he limps from the room, one hand cupping his side. The door slams shut behind him. There's the sound of a key turning.

My limbs are liquid, so I roll off the bed and crawl over to Talon. He pulls the knife free and chucks it across the floor. "Getting stabbed around you is becoming a habit." His voice is as shaky as my knees. Ruby-red blood is dripping down onto his shirt. I've never been good with blood. I shut my eyes against a room that is beginning to white out.

"Breathe," Talon says. "In through your nose. Out through your mouth."

I draw the air down into my lungs, pushing the dizziness away. After what feels like several centuries, the world stops spinning.

"Okay?"

I nod, and Talon sits back on his heels.

"He tried to— Scar tried to—"

"Yeah. He's a wanker."

"Is your face all right?"

"It's just a scratch." He pulls at the mask. "Wearing this thing all the time drives me crazy—"

"Don't take it off." I know how dangerous it would be for me to be able to identify these people.

Talon has tugged the mask farther down his face, as if to prove there is no way he is taking it off. "You weren't supposed to be treated like this. Everything is turning to shit."

"What's going to happen now?"

He turns his head to look at me. We are inches from each other, both our chests still heaving with adrenaline. As our eyes catch, the air between us cracks like a whip, with our anger at Scar . . . and . . . and something else. Something even more dangerous. I remember the way Talon sat with me when I cried. I remember the heat of his skin as it brushed against mine. And I draw in a deep, steadying breath, because I should not feel this way about him.

Talon's eyes flash pale green in the dim light. "Everything was so easy before," he says.

"Before what?"

"Before I met you."

"Oh."

"The way you stand up to Feather and Scar after every-thing you've been through. Shit, after everything *we've* put you through. You're so brave."

"I don't feel brave."

"Well, you are. It's all pretty messed up, isn't it?"

"What?"

"This. You . . . me. Robyn . . ."

Stop. I shouldn't be feeling like this. This isn't right.

My eyes flick away from his.

"Robyn," he says again. And this time it sounds harsh, like a broken promise. "Jesus, what the hell is the matter with me?"

With us.

At that moment, the door opens. We both tense. I tell myself it's because I'm afraid that Scar has come back for round two, but I know it's guilt at wanting to stay close to Talon. What kind of freak falls for her kidnapper?

Feather comes in. Her boots are muddy and covered in pine leaves. There must be a forest near the house. She takes in both of us. I can't see her face, but I imagine one eyebrow raises as she sees how close we are sitting together.

"Where is he?" Talon asks her.

"Calm down. He's upstairs." After stooping to pick up the knife, she puts it in her pocket.

"This is getting out of hand," Talon says.

"You think I don't know that? Are you all right?" she asks me brusquely, turning away before I have even finished nodding.

"Of course she's not!" Talon says. "I told you he can't be trusted. I told you, but you wouldn't listen."

"You talk a lot, Talon. It's kind of hard to pick out the important stuff. Anyway, it won't be a problem anymore. We're leaving. There's a man, a prison guard . . ." She glances at me. "I'll give you the details later. The point is that Scar's coming with me, so nothing will happen again."

I remember the hatred in Scar's eyes, and I don't believe her.

Feather and Scar left this morning. I heard the hum of an engine as I was doing my morning exercises. I tried to pinpoint the direction they were traveling in by the sound, but it was too difficult. People can only do that kind of stuff in films, I reckon. And besides, what would I do with the information anyway? It has been three days since Feather made that new video. What's happening out there? Have they reached a deal? The government must have promised something for me to still be alive. Maybe Feather has gone to meet the negotiator. But if they'd made a deal, she would have taken me with her.

Where the hell are the special-ops guys? Why haven't they smashed through the window of my cell and rescued me yet? Why am I still here?

Talon stays with me while I eat dinner. He did the same at breakfast and lunch. We didn't talk much then, either, so my chewing is awkwardly loud in the enclosed space. Talon doesn't seem to notice. He sits on the floor, like usual, resting against one wall, his legs splayed out in front of him, his head tilted up toward the window, as if he can feel the sun's rays through the glass. I drop the remaining half of the slice of bread back onto the plate, remembering the terror and revulsion of feeling Scar's body pressed against mine. What would have happened if Talon hadn't come in when he did? He protected me, and I should feel grateful. He's the only person who has been kind to me. I am glad he didn't get hurt. There's something calming about him, and besides, it is good to have someone to talk to. Yet I wouldn't be here if he hadn't kidnapped me. How can I have so many contradictory feelings associated with one person?

A sudden snap of wings from outside makes me jump. "I put some feed out for the birds this morning," Talon explains.

"Which ones did you see?"

"A few jays, a blackbird."

"I hear them singing sometimes, but I can't identify them from the book."

"Do you want to? I mean, I could teach you. Bird-watching is kind of sad, but it's not as though . . ."

"I'm doing anything else. Would we go outside?" I ask hopefully.

"No! We'd have to do it in here. But . . . wait." He disappears out of the cell and comes back a few minutes later with an iPod. He turns it on, and birdsong fills the room. "Dad used this to teach me and Jez."

Twiddle-oo twiddle-eedee.

"I know that one! That's a robin."

"Yeah, it's almost like I planned it."

I laugh. It's weird seeing glimpses of Talon's personality. He can be really funny sometimes.

Another robin joins in. They sound so cheerful, I can't help but smile.

"The sky's gray again today," Talon says, sitting cross-legged on the floor.

"The color of Bert the owl?"

"No, more like a sparrow. Here." He points to a page in the book as another bird joins in with the robins. "Right, let's get started. You have to close your eyes," he says as he shuts his. Looking at his eyelids feels like discovering a secret. There's a freckle in the crease of his right eye. As he opens his mouth to speak, his lips part slightly, making a noise like a kiss. Neither of us has mentioned what happened yesterday. Some things are too difficult to talk about.

"Can you hear it, the goldcrest?" he asks. "That high, thin note—*zi-zi-zi*. He's calling to his mate. There it is again." He whistles, his mouth forming a small O, and he sounds so real, so like a bird. "You try."

"I can't whistle."

He opens his eyes, lashes fluttering up like butterfly wings. "Of course you can. Everyone can whistle. You make a tunnel of your mouth. Push your lips forward like that. That's it. And then flatten your tongue. And—" The sound he makes is loud and pure, and exactly like a goldcrest's tweet.

"Why are you doing this?" I ask. "Being nice to me."

"It isn't right, what we've done."

"And you think teaching me to whistle makes up for that."

"Marble didn't shoot your dad, Robyn. I get that you probably won't believe me, but he is a good guy. There is no way he could shoot anyone. This whole thing is a mix-up. I wish there had been another way to clear it up, but there wasn't. We had to kidnap you and force your dad to take our requests for Marble to be freed seriously. You're his daughter. He'll fight hard for you. He'll make the government do it if he has to."

That's what I thought once. Now I'm not so sure. I don't say anything. I'm afraid of what will happen when Feather gets bored of waiting. I don't want to draw attention to my dad's lack of action. Not least because it hurts too much. Did he ever put me first, or was he just never forced to make a choice before?

"What's he like, your dad? I've only ever seen him on TV or in photos. He comes across as an arrogant dick. No offense."

I may be cross with Dad, but I won't bad-mouth him to Talon. "He isn't arrogant. He's confident. He has to be. Everyone expects him to know what to do."

"And are you a happy family like the press make out?"

Mum threw a plate at Dad last Christmas Eve. The tension had been building in the air all winter, like an electrical storm, and that day it broke right over our heads. *I can't do this anymore*, Mum had screamed, and then the crockery had come flying at Dad's head. It missed and clattered at his feet instead. Addy started to cry. "No fight," she said, banging her little fists on the table. Dad told her they weren't fighting; they were having a discussion. To which Mum retorted, "Discuss this," and then threw another plate at Dad's head. They made up the next day—well, as close to making up as my parents ever get. Just put a new sheet of paper over the crack in their marriage. Mum hates Downing Street—the cramped flat, the constant press invasion, the fact that Dad is never home when he says he will be—but there's nothing she can do about it.

Mum can throw every piece of crockery we own, including their wedding set, and it won't make the slightest bit of difference.

"Sometimes," I say. Suddenly I feel 180 years old.

"You do that a lot," he says. "Tug your hair forward."

He is right, I do, but I didn't realize I was doing it then. "I can't get used to it being this short." My hands tremble whenever I think of those scissors glittering in the bathroom light.

"Feather shouldn't have cut it. I don't know when everything got so messed up. The plan was simple: kidnap you. Get Marble back. Let you go. It makes me so mad when I think what they've both done to you. When I thought Scar was going to—"

"I'm pleased he isn't here anymore," I say quickly.

"I won't ever let him near you again. I won't let either of them hurt you again. I promise." There's such an intensity to his voice that I almost believe him.

Dad didn't make it to the Carter-Bresson museum today because Michael Bell, one of Dad's oldest friends, called to say that he was in Paris for the night before going on to Berlin and asked Dad to meet him for a late lunch. I don't know that Dad particularly wanted to, but he went anyway. He's weird like that about Michael sometimes. He always says it's because they've been friends for years, but I think it's more than that. I don't know what, but Dad gets really on edge around him. Mum reckons it was because Michael bullied Dad at school and he's been afraid of him ever since. She says it teasingly and goes on about heads down toilets and stuff like that, but I can't help thinking there is something else to it.

Anyway, so Dad went to meet Michael, and I tried not to feel grumpy about it. I obviously didn't do a very good job, because Gordon got one of his juniors to take me to the exhibition. He even took me out for a hot chocolate afterward, saying I had a face on me that would sour milk.

The meeting with the French president is planned for tomorrow afternoon; I'm flying home in the morning because spring term starts on Friday. Tonight Dad is going over some papers, and I'm lying on the sofa in the living room of the suite, watching *Road Runner* cartoons (there is literally nothing else on in English) and eating popcorn. Michael is, thankfully, elsewhere. Dad reaches for the popcorn, but I lift the bowl and wag a finger at him. "Na-huh. None for you, old man. Else you won't fit into those posh tailored suits."

"You really are a monster," he says.

I smile at him, half-chewed-up popcorn stuck in my teeth.

"It's been great having you with me these last few days. I know we don't often get much time together, just the two of us. I'm sorry that Michael turned up unexpectedly yesterday. Was the exhibition good?"

"Yes, it was amazing, and there was a temporary exhibition there as well. Lots of portraits . . ." I trail off. He's picked up a report from the table, and I can tell he's not really listening.

"Dad?"

"Hmm."

"You'll be careful the next few days, won't you?" No more has been said about the threat Gordon mentioned on the plane, but it's been on my mind.

"I'm meeting the French president, not going into battle. Although . . . some of these trade negotiations can get very bloody. I'll be careful. Don't you worry about me."

There's a knock on the suite door. "No rest for the wicked," Dad says with an apologetic wink, and goes to open it.

On the TV screen, Wile E. Coyote has just run over the edge of a cliff. His legs propel him forward for a few seconds until he realizes there is nothing below him. Then, with a look of resignation at the camera, his legs stop moving and he falls down the gorge. Dad's voice cuts through the closing credits. "Ah, Michael, hello, come in."

"Are you alone?"

"No, Bobs is here, but we're just watching cartoons. You wouldn't be—"

"I need to talk to you right now. Alone. It's that bastard Fletcher family. Sniffing around again. The son this time."

"Okay, well, calm down. Come in and we'll have a chat."

"We need to do more than that. They've got some journalist involved. She's got the whole damn story. Jesus Christ. This is such a mess."

"I wish you wouldn't always come to me with this, Michael. I can't be seen to—"

Michael says something too quietly for me to catch.

Dad's voice again. "Come in, then, but make it snappy."

Dad stalks back into the room, with Michael right behind him. A handful of papers are clutched in Dad's fist.

I am already sliding off the bed. "Something's come up. I know. I'm going."

"We'll catch up in the morning before your flight, I promise." Dad's voice is tight, and he doesn't take his eyes from the papers in his hand. Michael barely even nods at me. He flings his jacket down on one of the dining-room chairs.

As I slip my shoes on, popcorn spills out of the tub clutched under my arm.

"For God's sake, Robyn!" Dad snaps. "Be careful." He kicks the popcorn into a pile with the toe of one shoe. The papers in his hand flutter forward with the movement. Dad snatches them to him, but not before I see the words You have blood on your hands scrawled across the top in red ink.

CHAPTER ELEVEN

The lightbulb snaps on, spilling light over me. I have been sleeping fitfully. I half sit up. For a second, I am in the hospital in Paris, stretched out under a blanket on the couch in the nurses' station. It's very early in the morning, and I'm refusing to go home. I will not leave Dad until I know he's going to be okay. Until I know that he's going to live—

I blink, and I'm back in my white box.

Talon is standing over me. "We're going outside," he says.

My eyes flick to the tiny window. Gray cobwebs of sky signal that it is early, very early. But who cares? I haven't seen the sky in nine days. I am wide awake now and scrambling out of bed.

"You have to promise me you won't run," Talon says.

Lying takes only a second. "I promise."

The air is brittle and pierces my throat with every breath, but it is the most wonderful sensation ever. I am alive. I am breathing fresh air again. I don't care that it is predawn and freezing cold. I'm outside, somewhere I never thought I'd be again. Hard-packed earth is below me and there is a sky as clear and white as fresh snow above me.

Talon tied my hands behind my back, thankfully with a strip of fabric and not those horrible cable ties. My wrists are still tender and bruised from them. After walking up the now-familiar staircase from the basement into the kitchen, we headed down the corridor and out the front door, which opens onto a gravel driveway that disappears into a fence of trees. I was reminded again how different everything might have been if I'd turned left instead of right all that time ago.

Now Talon leads me around the side of the house—a large, two-story, white-stoned cottage, washed slate gray in the half-light. It is ugly and unkempt, with tiles missing from its roof. Grass and weeds push up between the stones of the tiny driveway, which is overhung on all sides by trees and hedges. Through a narrow gap between them I can just make out a road. The hedges continue around to the garden at the back of the house, beyond which are the beginnings of a wood. Bracken-covered paths weave through trees that are intricate black stencils against the lightening day.

No wonder no one has found me here. Why would anyone look in such a tiny, remote place?

We enter the wood. The first few trees are spread apart, but they quickly grow so closely together that there is barely any space between them. I try to listen for the sounds of cars that would suggest a road is nearby. There is nothing except for the occasional tweet of the birds in the shrubbery around us and our own breathing.

"Can you hear it? There's a bird—a sparrow, I think. Up in the tree behind you."

"You said you couldn't take me outside."

"I changed my mind."

We stop when we come to a partial break in the trees. There is a fallen log, and Talon gestures that we should sit down. Then he frees my hands. I flex my wrists to get the blood circulating. The trees are less dense here, and I can see a clearer way through them. I can now make out the dim, distant buzz of car engines. *This is it, Robyn. This is your chance to run.*

Talon lets go of my arm to take the rucksack off his back. *Move, Robyn.*

Talon's eyelashes are so long that they make shadows on his cheeks as he undoes the straps of the bag.

COME ON! MOVE! My body won't cooperate.

Talon looks up and smiles—I know this just from the crease at the corner of his eyes. He hands me an apple and a chunk of cheese. "Hungry?"

I take the food from him. I sit down next to him. I don't run.

There is a sudden snap of wings nearby, and I jump. Talon laughs. "Wimp," he says.

"Can you tell what they are?"

"From their wings flapping? Er . . . no."

"Call yourself a bird-watcher."

"Actually I'm a birder."

"A what?"

"Have I taught you nothing over the last week or so? Bird-watchers just watch birds. They don't really seek them out. They don't care that much what they see. Whereas birders are more picky."

"Like a connoisseur of birds."

"I'm going to ignore the sarcasm in your voice. We care about the environment and preserving it for future generations of birds."

"Both sound like stupid hobbies to me."

Talon smiles quickly, then says in a serious tone, "I want to tell you something. I've been thinking. Maybe if you know why I got involved in all this, then you might talk to your dad for me. I have no right to ask that, but I believe you're a good person, and if you knew what had happened to me, you might understand all this a bit more. You might help me."

He takes a photograph out of his pocket and flattens it out. It shows a dark-haired boy with a green eyes, like Talon's but not as bright. "That's my brother. It was taken about four years ago, so Jez would have been around ten. It was just before he got sick that last time. We'd gone to the beach for the day. Mum took that photo. She wanted one of both of us, but I kept ducking out of the way. See, there's my head." He unfolds the corner of the photo to reveal a blur of dark hair.

I lift the photo up so I can see it better. The boy—Jez—is grinning, chin pushed out in an exaggerated but real smile. "He looks nice."

"He was. You remember me telling you Jez got sick and died?"

"I remember."

"Well, it wasn't as simple as that. He had NFS, a kidney disease. He was born with it. It's hereditary. My parents were carriers, but it was recessive or something. Basically, neither of them knew they had it. 'A genetic lottery,' the doctors called it. There was, like, a one-in-four chance of their kids getting it. I don't have it. Jez did. It meant his kidneys didn't work properly. He was twelve when he died."

"I'm so sorry."

"No, listen. He didn't die of the disease. The disease was bad, yes, but he was doing okay. Amazingly okay. He had to have dialysis and it was shit, but he was going to get a new kidney. He and I were a perfect match. I was going to give him one of my kidneys, and he would have been all right." He takes the photo back from me; the edges crumple as his hand fists.

"Then . . . ?"

"My brother didn't just die. He was murdered by the head of Bell-Barkov, Michael Bell, and your dad helped cover it up."

• • •

The two men go into Dad's study. Dad's face is white. I can't get those words out of my mind: You have blood on your hands. *It is the only excuse I can give for what I do next. After waiting a few minutes to let them get well and truly into the conversation, I creep down the hall beside the study and into the bathroom on the other side of it. Then I open the window and pray that Dad hasn't shut the one in his office.*

Michael is speaking. ". . . journalist sniffing around for weeks. We got the police onto her. Restraining order, the lot. The coppers have been very good about that sort of thing since that fire last year. This time it hasn't done any good. She's still been hanging around, hassling my staff and asking all manner of questions, about our animal-testing program and our work in Nigeria. How much do we pay those who volunteer for testing over there? Are they fully aware of the risks involved? Now she's got wind of that incident a couple of years back. Even got hold of the voice-mail message I left you. Sent this ridiculously incendiary photo of a kid and a rabbit. Going on and on about our drugs' testing procedures, how we use animals and this, that, and the other. Inadequate staffing. The lot. We are about to get regulatory approval for the drug to go international. I can't have anything messing with that. I need you to do something. Put pressure on someone."

"Like who? What do you want me to do?" Dad sounds incredulous.

"*Come on. You're up to your neck in this, Stephen, just like me. Do you think the public will be impressed to learn that you knew about the issues with this drug and did nothing because you needed some extra cash?*"

I have been resting on the windowsill, and I'm so shocked by what Michael's just said that I lean too far out. In my scramble not to fall, I knock the flowerpot off the sill. It turns over and over, spraying petals, and then smacks against the tarmac on the courtyard below.

"*What was that?*" *Michael says, and before I have time to duck back inside, he is at the window next to me. He looks quickly down and then right, at me. His face masks into a purple rage, and I duck back inside. Every instinct is telling me to run, to not let him catch me. After tugging open the bathroom door, I scoot down the corridor toward my room, but Michael is fast. There is a hand on my shoulder. Michael spins me around, digging his hands into my upper arms.* "*You little bitch, you were listening!*" *His face is red with rage, and each word is punctuated with spittle.*

"*I—I—I—*"

He shakes me. "*Tell me what you heard!*"

Dad's voice thunders down the corridor. "*GET AWAY FROM MY DAUGHTER.*"

Michael steps back, his skin already turning white. He looks at his hands as if he can't believe what he has just done. Dad puts his arms around me, but I push him away.

I don't know why, but I'm angry and scared.

"I think it's best if you go, Michael," Dad says.

Michael nods. He is so white now I'm afraid he will pass out. Using one hand to steady himself, he stumbles down the hall like a drunk.

"You took money from Michael." I am so angry that my hands are shaking. "For what? What drugs is he talking about?"

"You need to calm down." Dad takes a step toward me.

"Don't come any closer!" I yell. "I don't want you anywhere near me!" I don't understand what's going on, but instinct tells me that Dad has done something wrong.

His eyes narrow as the politician replaces the father. "You will calm down this instant. You are hysterical. You had no right listening at doors. No right, whatsoever. Now, get back to your room."

"No. Tell me what you were talking about."

"I am your father and I am the British prime minister and I am telling you not to meddle in things you do not understand. You have no idea what you are getting involved in." His skin is mottled white and pink, contorted with so much anger that I don't even recognize him.

I back away from him, because for the first time in my life, I'm scared of what my dad is capable of.

CHAPTER TWELVE

"Sorry, *what?*" My voice is very small, like the tinkle of glass when it breaks.

"Jez was killed by Amabim-F, Bell-Barkov's new wonder drug for treating kidney failure. Only it wasn't wonderful. It was poisonous. It was early on, during the clinical trials. His doctor said there was this new drug that would somehow fix Jez's kidneys. I thought it was bullshit, but my parents . . . and Jez . . . they wanted to go for it.

"Jez was the sweetest kid ever. He hated the thought of me giving up my kidney for him. He wanted to try. . . ." Talon's eyes are misty, and he swipes his hand quickly across his face. "He wanted to try it. I begged him not to. Who really knew what that shit would do to the body? He was a stubborn bugger, though. Insisted. And . . . and . . ." His eyes fill again, and this time he doesn't bother to wipe the tears away. "He died. Anaphylactic shock."

"But Jez was sick. You said yourself that there was no cure. It was an accident. Not murder."

"Bell-Barkov *knew* there were side effects. Jez wasn't the only one who got sick. Bell-Barkov had messed up the trials from the beginning. A lot of the animals they tested on suffered allergic reactions. And a monkey actually died, but no one took any notice. Or they turned a blind eye. Blamed it on the fact that animals have a completely different genetic makeup from humans; testing on them can only prove so much. That's one of the reasons Feather is so against animal testing. It doesn't give the results scientists say it does, so the animals are just being tortured for no reason."

"What are you saying? Animals got sick? Did any other people get ill too?" I ask, trying to keep my voice from trembling. Michael's words are coming back to me: *Journalist sniffing around . . . Going on and on about our drugs' testing procedures, how we use animals and this, that, and the other.*

"Some of the earlier patients on the trials—the ones who didn't have kidney failure—had bad symptoms. Allergic reactions. Swellings. They weren't reported properly. Another man died. He was older than Jez. It's hard to work out if it was because of the drug or not. We suspect it was just covered up too, like Jez's death was." He pulls a couple of other sheets of paper from his pocket. "These are various reports from doctors about the different side effects."

"There would have been an investigation." None of this is true. It can't be.

"There was, and it said that Jez died of an 'underlying

condition.' Dad fought the result of the hearing. Made himself sick with all the research. He and Mum were arguing all the time. She couldn't understand why getting Bell-Barkov to admit that there was a problem with the drug mattered. It wasn't like it was going to bring Jez back. But it does matter! These people are still free to hurt other kids. Other people. Bell-Barkov wanted to discredit Dad. They didn't want anything to get in the way of producing and marketing this drug. Development costs a fortune, but then a lot of money can be made from new medicines once they are on the market, especially something like this that could potentially cure kidney disease."

"It's so sad what happened to your family, but—"

"You don't get it yet, do you? Bell-Barkov is willing to do almost anything to keep this stuff quiet. Even set fire to their own premises."

"What?"

"The fire at Bell-Barkov last October. Bit convenient, don't you think?"

"That was the AFC."

"No, it wasn't. Bell-Barkov are experts at covering their tracks. Intimidation, bribery. Whatever works. Mum got mugged one night on the way back from the tube. Only after taking her wallet, the guy told her to keep her husband under control. 'Stop him sticking his nose in places it isn't wanted.' She and Dad had a screaming row that night. She told him to leave; he was putting us all in danger with his crazy conspiracy stories. When we woke up the next day, Dad was gone. They found his body a couple of weeks later, washed up on a beach in Dorset."

"He killed himself?" I can barely believe what I'm hearing.

"Yeah, or maybe he'd stuck his nose too far into a place it wasn't wanted. I don't know. I'm not trying to make this into a ridiculous conspiracy. That's Feather's job. Whether it was something more sinister, or just Dad having had enough, it was still Bell-Barkov's fault. They killed my dad, just like they killed my brother."

"And you think Michael—Mr. Bell—knew about all this?" I ask, even though I already know the truth.

"We know he knew about Jez. We've got a voice mail of him freaking out about it. On it, he admits that there were issues before. They were kept quiet, though, presumably because of the amount of money they'd already invested in the drug."

My throat is tight, as if I'm trying to breathe through plastic. This is not the first time I have talked about this.

"The message was left on your dad's voice mail. He kept quiet about it for whatever reason. Money, possibly. We know that Bell-Barkov gave a lot to his election campaign. Or maybe it was because him and Michael were friends, or just because it wouldn't look good for him to be so close to this kind of scandal."

You're up to your neck in this, Stephen, just like me. It can't be true. Dad *promised* me.

"Feather is lying to you, Talon. Can't you see that?" I say desperately. "She's convinced you that my dad and Michael are involved in some crazy cover-up. Listen to yourself, though. It is insane. She wanted you to help get her brother out of prison, so she's told you a load of rubbish to try to connect the two things. How messed up is that?"

"I thought you were better than this. Why would I lie to you? What have I got to gain? Don't you think your dad has more to lose by people thinking his best friend—the man who helped pay for his campaign—is involved in a kid's death? But no, you couldn't believe your dad was lying. Even though he has done it before. To you."

"When?"

"The whole country saw it. It was on national TV. When he promised he was doing everything he could to bring you home. Well, where is he, Robyn? Why hasn't he let Marble go? That was all he had to do and you'd be home by now."

"SHUT. UP. You don't know anything about my father." I stand up, fists curled at my sides, as though ready for a fight. But I'm tired of fighting. I just want this to be over. I don't want to hear anything else Talon has to say, so I start to run, like I should have done a long, long time ago.

I head in the direction of the road, reaching the first line of trees in seconds, and then I am weaving through them as fast as I can over the uneven terrain. I am trying to ignore the small voice inside my head that is telling me to go back. I have been running from what happened in Paris for three months, and I am running still. Talon is a liar and a kidnapper. I owe him nothing. I have to use every opportunity I can to escape.

Talon is right behind me now. I can just make out his footfalls over the rasp of my own breath and the crunch of dead leaves beneath my feet. Up ahead I see a break in the trees, and I lengthen my strides and swing my arms to propel myself toward it. The quiet hum of traffic is louder and more insistent. It can't be much farther now. If I can just make that next clearing, I reckon I'll be able to see the road—

I don't make it.

I trip, catching my foot on a tree root that's twisted like a pretzel, and go down hard. Talon is on me the instant I hit the ground. Instinctively, I curl up into a ball, but he lets go of me immediately and sits back on his heels. There is only stillness and quiet.

I peer up at him and see that there is no anger in his eyes, only . . . only . . . *disappointment*. He doesn't look like a kidnapper. He looks like a boy who's been betrayed by someone he trusted.

"You promised me you wouldn't run," he says.

I don't move. I don't speak. Shame burns through me, followed by anger, because I don't want to care about this boy. When did everything get so complicated?

Since I stopped believing everything my father tells me.

Talon begins to pull his mask up over his face.

"No!" I cry. "Don't."

He ignores me. His face is revealed a section at a time: first a pointed chin, then soft lips, sloping cheekbones, and finally those dark-green eyes that I already know so well. They seem to sparkle now in the sun-dappled shade of the clearing. He is younger than I expected, only a few years older than me. My treacherous heart begins to beat a little faster. Even after everything that's happened, I want to reach out and touch his face, run my fingers along his chin, his lips, up across the bridge of his eyebrows. What is wrong with me? This is the boy who kidnapped me; the one who is telling lies about my dad.

"I don't know why I ever got involved in this. Jez would be ashamed of me," Talon says.

And I read in his eyes that he has finally realized that nothing good was ever going to come of kidnapping me. It was never going to bring his brother back. It was only going to cause more misery. I think of Addy and how I'd feel if anything ever happened to her, and I understand being so angry and so mad with grief that you lose all common sense and do something stupid, because you would do anything to just stop the pain inside you for a second. For half a second.

"I am not your kidnapper now," he says, dropping the mask on the ground. "I'm just Samuel Fletcher, and I'm telling you the truth about what happened to my brother."

It's just gone ten-thirty a.m. My plane leaves in two hours, and Dad is due at a press conference in half an hour. He's already knocked on my door three times this morning, the first for breakfast, the second to say he'd saved me a pain au chocolat, the third to say he was leaving soon. "Bobs," he said through the wood. "Please, come and talk to me."

I ignored him.

I am lying curled up in bed, the duvet pulled over my head, hiding like a little kid. I know that there is more to yesterday's conversation. You do not attack the daughter of your best friend over a misunderstanding.

The sound of voices is coming from the living room; I should get up or I'll miss the plane. Instead I press a pillow over my head. I just want everyone to go away. I don't care if I miss my plane. I'll stay here forever. I'm never going home. I'll move to Paris. Get a job.

I am being stupid and childish, but I let the thought run. I could work at the Louvre or in a little bakery, and I'd have a flat that overlooked the Seine. I wouldn't have much money, but that would be okay. I could take photos, loads of photos, and then I could sell them. Or even talk to an art gallery about displaying them. Perhaps I would become famous? Loads of photographers started out taking pictures of Paris. It is the most beautiful, most romantic city in the world.

My thoughts are cut off by the sound of Gordon's voice

coming down the corridor. I slide out of bed, which means I am standing when he knocks sharply on the door before opening it. "Sorry to disturb you, Robyn, but we need to leave immediately."

"What's going on?"

Gordon is already hustling me down the corridor and into the living room. "We have reason to believe—"

"It's nothing to worry about," Dad says. He is by the long dining table, piling some papers into a briefcase.

"What is nothing to worry about? Tell me!"

After a nod from Dad, Gordon answers, "We have reason to believe that there is a bomb in the hotel."

"Oh my God. When? How?"

"Robyn, we don't want you to be scared. There was an anonymous tip-off. We doubt it is a real threat, but we must take these things seriously. We need to leave now."

"I'm in my pajamas," I say idiotically. There might be a bomb in the hotel. My brain can't seem to process the information.

"Lucky they are your best ones, then." Dad smiles while Gordon wraps the throw from the sofa around my shoulders.

"You should bring a jacket too, sir."

"They are all in the bedroom. No need."

"It might be best to cover your face, Prime Minister."

"Oh, fine, fine. I can't see that there is anything to worry about." Michael Bell's disgusting brown jacket with dark mustard-yellow patches on the elbows is still on the back of one of the chairs. Dad picks it up as Gordon hurries us from the room.

The hall is full of police, the lift waiting for us at the end of it. The blanket around my shoulders smells faintly of popcorn. I think of Wile E. Coyote running off the edge of the cliff, his legs propelling him onward until he realizes there is nothing below him, and then he just drops. Dad and Gordon stand on either side of me in the lift. I can't believe this is happening. Who wants to blow up the hotel? Do they want to hurt Dad? Why? Has this got something to do with what he and Michael were talking about last night?

You're up to your neck in this, Stephen.

The lift pings. The doors open, and the hotel atrium is before us, marble and gold with a set of revolving doors that head outside. I'm scared.

"Dad," I whisper. "Dad, I—I—"

Dad isn't listening, though, and Gordon is pushing me forward, one hand on my back. "Nothing to worry about," he says. "The car is right there. Pull that blanket over your head, Robyn. That's it. And Prime Minister, if you could do the same, sir. Thank you. We ask that you walk calmly but quickly to the car."

Calmly.

I don't feel calm. Why is Dad walking so quickly? Wait! Wait for me.

I speed-walk a couple of paces to keep up with him, so that we emerge onto the hotel steps together. "Quickly but calmly, Robyn," Dad says. "Just like Gordon—"

Thwack! A noise like a tennis ball hitting a racket. What the hell . . . ?

Someone shouts, "Get down!" But it's all happening too fast, and I don't understand what is going on. A police officer goes to push my dad to the ground, but Dad throws his body over mine instead. There's another dull thwack, and Dad shudders. At first I think it's because we've landed awkwardly after tumbling down the hotel steps. I roll over, sliding out from underneath him. Dad doesn't move. Blood is soaking through the shoulder of Michael's jacket, staining the snow as crimson as a summer sunset.

"Dad! DAD!"

He doesn't hear me; he is already losing consciousness.

My heart is thudding loudly in my ears—durdum durdum durdum—matching the pace of the blood that is pouring out onto the snow.

Durdum. Durdum. Durdum. My heart beats loud in my ears, like it did on the day Dad was shot.

Red blood on white snow.

You're up to your neck in this, Stephen.

Tell me, Dad. What have you done?

"All I want is a proper investigation," Talon says. "That

drug killed my brother, and I don't want it to happen to anyone else."

"It won't because it's a lie." *Is it?* My doubt makes me angry, so I lash out at the cause of it. "You just don't want to admit that you had no reason to kidnap me. Dad isn't going to release Marble. He's a murderer!" As I say it, I finally realize that Dad isn't coming for me. How can he set a terrorist free?

You're up to your neck in this, Stephen.

I duck my head to let my hair drop around me, like a cocoon, but there isn't enough to hide me now.

"I'm going to let you go," Talon says.

"You are?"

"Yeah. The road is only fifteen minutes in that direction. You'll be able to hitch a lift from there."

"Thank you! I can't believe it." Relief floods through me; I don't have to think about any of this anymore.

"Just do me a favor and ask your dad about the voice mail. Ask him a proper question for once, Robyn."

For once. Am I a stuck-up princess? Am I naive to still believe what my dad told me? I don't want to think about the answers to those questions. The important thing now is that I'm free. All of this is over. I'm going home.

Dad is in intensive care for three days. One of the bullets had grazed him, but the worst of his injuries was to the left shoulder joint. The entry wound was small, only about a centimeter in diameter. There was no exit wound, and the damage caused was extensive. The bullet had taken out most of his scapula and clavicle. Metallic fragments had punctured his left lung and scattered all over the front of his chest. The doctors gave him a blood transfusion and pumped him full of intravenous penicillin. All these phrases—scapula, entry wound, transfusion—trip off my tongue so easily now.

Two days ago they moved him to a high-dependency unit. Mum arrived sometime during the night of the day it happened. She has been by his side almost all the time. I have barely left the hospital, but I haven't been in to see him. Not really. I have peered in through glass windows and peeked around curtains, lurking in the background and retreating like a shadow at noon. I am embarrassed, afraid, angry.

Today he has asked to see me.

It is dark when I arrive, but he is still up, sitting in the day chair, his shoulder in a fresh bandage. His head is resting against the back of the chair, his eyes closed. The only light comes from the hallway and the streetlamps outside. I hesitate in the doorway. The nurses told Mum that he hasn't been sleeping well. He ran a high temperature yesterday. I don't want to disturb him unnecessarily. Before I can make up my mind about whether to stay or run away again, he opens his eyes and sees me. "Robyn! Come in."

I cross the room slowly, feeling awkward with him for the second time in my life. Outside, the snow has begun to melt.

I am leaving wet footprints on the clean linoleum floor. I stop halfway across the room, suddenly unable to go any farther. "Were you sleeping?" I ask. "I could come back. . . ."

He is surrounded by more machines than the entire MI5 office—one monitoring his breathing, one his morphine, one his heart. They match the rhythm of my own heartbeat.

He smiles. "I wasn't sleeping. I was waiting for you. Come and sit down. Don't loiter by the door."

There is a chair opposite him and I sit down in it, playing with my sleeve. My hair falls into my eyes. Silence stretches out between us, as wide as the Grand Canyon.

"Did you think he was aiming at me? Is that why you protected me?"

"If a man is shooting a gun anywhere near your daughter, you don't wait to see where it's pointing. My first instinct will always be to protect you."

"You could have died."

"But I didn't." He smiles again. "I can hear your brain ticking over, Bobs. We have unfinished business, you and I. I hoped I had brought you up to understand that it is impolite to eavesdrop, but what you overheard and then Michael's reaction . . . It frightened me, and I may not have acted correctly. I should have told you the truth immediately."

"Did you take money from Michael to keep quiet about something?"

"There are some things that are more complicated than

they seem. Bell-Barkov invested billions into our country at a time when we had record levels of unemployment."

"Did you take money from them?"

"No. Michael gave me a loan during the election campaign, but it was as a friend. Nothing to do with Bell-Barkov whatsoever, and I have paid him back in full."

"What were you supposed to be covering up?"

Dad sighs. "About two years ago, a little boy on one of Bell-Barkov's drug-testing programs got very sick and tragically died. It was not Michael's fault and none of his staff were to blame, but understandably the boy's parents were upset, and there was a bit of a fuss. Michael was in a terrible state. He left a message on my voice mail, garbled and slightly hysterical, saying that the drug was responsible. He believed at the time that the boy had reacted badly to some aspect of it and that he was to blame. Of course he wasn't."

"And someone got hold of that message?"

"An unscrupulous journalist, yes. Or a private eye, who then passed it on to the papers. Now his family are being encouraged to believe that there is more to it. The AFC have been after Michael for some time. Death threats, arson attacks."

"The fire at his office last year?"

"We believe so—and now with this assassination attempt, it seems they have shifted focus to me. Killing a prime minister would certainly get you more news coverage."

I flinch at his choice of words but force myself to go on.

"On some papers that Michael gave you were the words 'You have blood on your hands.' I thought they were talking about animal testing, but they weren't. It was a kid."

"It is a tragic, terrible case of a child dying and his parents' grief being used by a group of people wanting to cause trouble."

"But Michael was so angry!"

"Wouldn't you be, if you'd been accused of killing a child? But there is no excuse for how he reacted. We don't yet know who fired the shots last Thursday, but we believe it was the AFC. They have been targeting Michael's company on and off over the years, for numerous incorrect assumptions: illegal drug testing, their use of animals in testing, and so forth. We believe they called in the bomb threat at the hotel and then took a shot at me. They are angry about my friendship with Michael."

"But it makes no sense! Blow stuff up and kill people to protect animal and human rights?"

"Extremism rarely makes sense. Everyone in my government is working hard to come up with a lasting solution to end this terror. But all it takes is for one terrorist to get lucky once. The police and the defense units have to be lucky all the damn time. And sometimes the information we need isn't easy to come by. There is no denying that drug testing is a complex and sensitive moral issue, one that there isn't an easy solution to, but being in charge is all about making tough decisions. Decisions that no one else wants to make, and we will be judged for those decisions. We are, after all, the choices we make. I have never told a soul about that voice mail from Michael. I know he frightened you the other day, but he's frightened too. There is a lot at stake here."

"Is the journalist who sent you this stuff going to publish a story?"

"No. She doesn't want to be connected with a terrorist organization, and after"—he nods at his shoulder—"I'd like to think this conversation will remain between us, Robyn."

"I won't tell anyone. I—I don't like Michael much right now, but I trust you, so I won't say anything. I mean, what would I say anyway? Michael didn't kill that kid. He didn't have anything to do with it. I believe you."

Do I? Dad's hospital room is darker now. The streetlamps have to work harder to pierce the gloom. I stand up and go over to the window. Outside I can just make out the tops of the nearby trees. One branch is closer than all the others, its gnarled fingers reaching out to strike the pane. The clouds have lifted and the sky is bare and dark, ice-white stars dim against the brightly colored halo of the city lights. I stare deep into the cold, dark sky until my eyes burn. Dad nearly died, and he's still in a lot of pain. I don't want us to argue anymore. What do I know about any of this, anyway? I force any last niggling doubts away and then, turning back into the warm light of the hospital room, I ask, "What was the boy's name? The one who died?"

"What does that matter?"

"It just feels important. I know it wasn't anyone's fault that he died, but it is still sad, and it feels right to name him."

"Yes, yes, you're probably right, my darling." There's a glass of water on the table beside my dad. He gestures for it, and I pass it to him. He takes a long, slow sip before holding the glass out for me to return it. When he does so, I notice that his hand is shaking. Still he doesn't answer. It is only after I've sat back down that he says quietly and slowly, as if weighing something, "The child's name was Jeremy. Jeremy Fletcher, I believe."

It starts raining soon after I leave Talon. I promised myself that if I ever got the chance to run, I would, but to leave him there in that clearing, to not even look back, was harder than I thought it would be. The forest floor is wet now and slippery, and the sky is dark with more rain. Trees pack in tightly all around me, but I can hear the road more clearly.

Talon's real name is Samuel Fletcher. His brother is Jez—Jeremy Fletcher. It is the boy Dad told me about in Paris. I should be glad that I know Talon's name. It will make it easier for the police to catch him. Instead I am sad that it was his family the AFC manipulated and used for their own ends. If they'd left him alone, Talon would never have kidnapped me.

I push into the breeze and begin to walk slowly up the road, keeping to the shallow ditch on one side. The rain doesn't let up, socking me in the face with drops that feel the size of a baby's fist. It feels wonderful. I'm free! Finally. In a few hours, I could be home with Mum and Addy. And Dad.

You're up to your neck in this, Stephen.

There's the distant roar of an engine, and I shake myself free of the thought. As the car turns a corner, I begin to wave my arms and yell at the driver to stop. Lights and a blaring horn blast into me as the driver swerves and disappears into the distance. "Come back!" I shout, flinging a stone after the departing vehicle. It bumps once in the road and then drops down into the ditch. On the other side of the road, the wood stretches on and on into what might as well be eternity. It doesn't matter. I don't even care that I'm soaking wet and starting to shiver. I'm outside in the rain, under the sky, and I can hear birds singing and I can see the trees.

I walk on for what must be another half hour at least. Not a single car has passed by. The initial euphoria of being free has evaporated. I'm giving in to the cold. My teeth are chattering, and my brain keeps playing that conversation with Talon over and over. I'm so distracted that I almost don't notice the shadow of the tree trunks lengthen as a car approaches with its headlights on. I am taking no chances. I stand right in the center of the road and swing my arms in a huge arc. The driver honks his horn, but that only makes me wave more.

"Stop!" I shout. "Please, stop!"

The car steers sharply to the right to avoid me, then pulls to a stop a little farther down the road.

I run toward the vehicle, which is actually more of a van. It looks dirty in the heavy rain, but in true light, it would be white. I slow my pace, feet tripping over each other.

I know this van.

I take a step back, and then another as the door opens. But it is already too late. A man is climbing out, and even in the rain-washed half-light, I can see that he is huge. He pulls something long and dark out of the van's front seat and holds it up. It's a gun. Its shiny surface winks at me, as though it knows a secret.

Scar is standing on the road in front of me, a rifle in his hands.

CHAPTER THIRTEEN

"Did they hurt you?" Talon asks.

"Apart from tying me to a bed again, no." We've both been bound by cable ties to opposite ends of the bed in my old cell. After I so helpfully flagged down the van, Scar had easily bundled me into the back of it, and then he and Feather drove me back here to the farmhouse. Talon had come outside as we'd pulled up in the driveway.

"Lose something?" Feather asked him as she climbed out of the van. At her command, Scar dragged me from the vehicle and dumped me on the gravel at Talon's feet. Before Talon could reply, Feather stalked the distance between them and smacked him in the jaw.

It is still raining heavily, and streams of water pour down the windowpane. It's windy too, and a branch or something is being whipped rhythmically against the glass.

"What will they do with us?" I ask.

"I don't know." He slides his foot along the floor until his leg is resting against my ankle. I can feel the warmth of him through my tracksuit bottoms. "It'll be okay. We'll be okay."

But when the bough of the tree slams into the glass again, making it vibrate against the frame, we both jump, and I know he is afraid too.

"What if Scar . . . ?"

"I won't let him anywhere near you," he says fiercely. His left cheek is bright red from where Feather hit him, and she's tiny. We really don't stand a chance against Scar. It means a lot that he is determined to fight with me, though, even after our conversation in the forest about my dad. I don't want to bring that up again. I don't want to see the look of disappointment on his face.

"Where have they been since yesterday?" I ask instead.

"They went to see this guy who used to work as a prison guard at the place Marble is being kept. He reckons he can help them get him out. Some kind of prison break. Shit. I don't know. The whole thing sounds insane."

"But if Dad . . . if Dad isn't negotiating with them, then . . . then there's no reason to keep me alive. Is that why you let me go? Because you thought they were going to . . . hurt me?"

"I'm sure Feather would never . . . But she's changed. She won't listen to me anymore. She spends all this time with Scar, and he's bad, Robyn. Really bad. His ex-girlfriend went missing a few years back, and there was a rumor he . . . you know."

"Killed her?"

"I don't know. But there's something wrong with him. You've seen his fingers? Who does that to themselves? And he doesn't care about Marble or Jez or animal welfare, or any of the other stuff Feather and I do. He just likes to break things and hurt people."

I open my mouth to tell him about my conversation with Dad when he was in the hospital. I want him to understand that it's Feather and Scar who are wrong. They are lying, not my dad. The sound of the bolt being drawn back stops me.

Feather opens the door and steps into the cell. She's cast in light like some kind of avenging angel. Talon says her name, but Feather cuts right through him. "Shut your mouth. I'm not here to talk to you. It's all agreed, Princess. You're going home. We're getting Marble back." She crouches over Talon and grabs a handful of his T-shirt. "I will never forgive you for what you've done." I draw back my leg, ready to kick her if she hits him again. She stands up, though, and her voice is controlled as she says, "I hate you for this." With the light behind her and her face in shadow, it takes a second to realize she was talking to me.

With a blanket over my head, I am led from the van. We set off from the house at about lunchtime. Talon and I had been left chained up in the cell all night, with no food or water. Feather gave us a couple of stale bread rolls and a bottle of water this morning. That was hours ago, though, and I'm especially thirsty after being locked in the back of the windowless, airless van. As our hands were cuffed behind our backs, we couldn't hold on to anything properly and were bumped and battered against the metal walls. Eventually Talon managed to wedge himself in one corner by pressing one leg against the right wall of the van and the other against the curve of metal that covered the wheel. He told me to sit in between his legs and hold on to his T-shirt. "At least then you'll bump against my legs rather than the wall." It felt too intimate to sit that close to him, but after knocking my head against the metal for the third time, I finally agreed. Holding on to him was really difficult, and after a while my hand ached too much.

"Just lean against me," he said. "I mean, it's okay, if you want to." I leaned back slowly. I could feel the tension in his body too, but also the warmth of him, and the steady beat of his heart was soothing. My own was racing. I should have had more faith in Dad. Of course he couldn't announce on national TV that he was going to release a known terrorist, but he's obviously been working with the police and Parliament to get it sorted.

Feather pushes me forward now with a sharp jab to my spine. I'm bundled up some steps. I stumble over the last one, banging my knee painfully against the ground, and into some sort of building, then up more stairs and along a corridor. We stop as a door is unlocked, and she shoves me down a shorter hallway, across a room, and finally knocks me to the floor.

"Move and I'll cut your throat," Feather says after securing my handcuffs to a radiator. I expect to hear her footsteps crossing the floor, but instead she grabs me roughly by the chin and rips the blanket from my face. I'm staring into her cold, dark eyes. "You might have tricked Talon into believing you give a shit about our cause, but not me. I know you just played him so you had a chance to escape."

Talon is brought into the room then by Scar. He is pushed down next to me and Scar binds him to the same radiator, pulling the cuffs tight, so they bite into Talon's skin. Then Feather ties something around my eyes, and I can't see anything else. "If I hear so much as a squeak out of either of you, I'll lock Scar in here with you," she says.

Scar laughs. "Any excuse," he says. "Any excuse."

"Feather, can't we talk about this—," Talon begins.

"I'm done talking with you," Feather says. "Now shut your mouth and keep it shut." I hear her and Scar cross the room, then the sound of a door opening and closing, and finally a key turning in a lock.

"Well," Talon whispers, "I guess this is marginally better than the van. At least the walls are no longer trying to knock us out."

"Where are we?" I ask. It's horrible not being able to see.

"I don't know. Another safe house, one closer to the hand-over point, probably."

"Which is . . . ?"

"'Cause they'd definitely tell me that."

"You're angry with me?"

"With you? No. Not really. A bit. I thought you'd listen to me, but you just kept defending your dad."

"Because he's my *dad*. You have to understand that, surely?"

"But he's been lying to you."

"Not about everything. He wasn't lying about doing anything to get me back, like you said he was. He's releasing Marble."

"He took his time about it."

There's no denying that, but I don't want to talk about it. "Do you think you can do one bad thing and still be a good person?" I ask.

Talon sighs. "No one is ever just one thing. It takes a whole lifetime of decisions to make you who you are."

"'We are the choices we make.'"

"What?"

"It's just something my dad said once." The night he told me that Jez hadn't died because of Michael's drug, but I don't tell Talon that. "How did you know about the voice-mail message?"

"Feather. She'd been working with a journalist to uncover some of the dodgy animal-testing programs at Bell-Barkov, and they came across it."

"They hacked into my dad's voice-mail messages, you mean."

"So what? Your dad and Michael are best friends. There was a chance Michael would talk to him about what was going on."

"How did you get involved in all of it?"

"Dad had been in contact with Feather. I don't know if she got in touch with him or the other way around. Anyway, after he died, she called up. Said she had some stuff on Bell-Barkov if I was interested. And of course I was. I was a mess after Dad and Jez died. Mum was even worse. I couldn't stand being at home. Feather had a flat with Marble in London. Their parents died in a car accident a few years before and left them some cash. She got what I was going through. Said she wanted to help me. Said we could work together to bring Bell-Barkov down. And it appealed to me. I felt like I'd found not only how to fight but someone to do it with."

"And Marble, too?"

"Not really. He didn't get what Feather was trying to do with the AFC. He just wanted to go on marches and lobby for better conditions for animals in labs. He thought Feather was too aggressive with Bell-Barkov. He worried about her getting arrested. It became difficult living in the flat. We'd argue a lot. Feather can be brilliant, passionate, but she's moody as hell. On her bad days, me and Marble would be walking on eggshells around her. She believes in total equality: woman, man, animal, tree, plant. Anything that exists basically should be valued and protected. By violent means if necessary. She couldn't understand how getting justice for Jez meant more to me than animal welfare. She called it 'personal campaigning.' You're doing it because it does something good for you, when in actual fact anything you do should be selfless and for the common good."

"But you still helped her? You still kidnapped me?"

"Marble is my friend, and he's innocent."

"How can you be so sure about that?"

"Because he was with me when your dad was shot. We were in the flat, playing video games all afternoon."

"Why didn't you tell the police that?"

"I have! Loads of times. Marble keeps telling them I'm lying. He's obviously covering for someone or something. I don't know."

And it hasn't occurred to Talon who that person might be. "Where was Feather that day?"

"Out with Scar somewhere. . . No, oh no. She wouldn't. She couldn't have done. I know Feather and there's no way."

I thought there was no way my dad would ever lie to me.

My arms are hurting; I try to shift into a more comfortable position.

"I was angry and desperate when we took you captive. One of my best friends was in jail, facing a life sentence for something he didn't do. My brother and my dad were dead. My mum was going crazy with grief. But I swear if I thought for a single second that Feather had—had tried to kill someone, there is no way I would have got involved in this."

I try again to move into a more comfortable position, fail, and say, "I don't want to talk about this anymore. Talk to me about something else. Anything. Let's just pretend for two seconds that we're not tied to a radiator, that we're in café, drinking hot chocolate. We've just met because there are no other tables and so you have to share mine."

His voice is full of emotion. "You want to imagine meeting me somewhere else?"

Do I? There are too many questions I don't want to answer in that sentence. "I want to imagine being somewhere else. But you can't talk about birds. Not spotting them, watching them, or pretending to be them. Okay?"

"I do have other topics of conversation, you know."

"Like badgers? Dolphins? Fish?"

"Okay, Little Miss Interesting, you choose a topic."

"A favorite day. Tell me about your best memory."

"That's easy. The beach at Brighton the summer before Jez died. Your turn."

"Christmas this year. I got a digital camera. Addy had wrapped it in brown paper that she'd covered in stickers. And

I mean, *covered* it in stickers. It looked like the glitter monster had had a serious case of diarrhea. Anyway, she started crying as soon as I took the paper off and she realized that her paper wasn't the present. I had to pretend all afternoon that it was. But it was kind of special, really. She's silly, my sister, but I like how easy she is to please and that she thinks I'm, like, the best person ever."

"How old is she?"

"Three. She'll be four in September. I know it's weird her being so much younger. I don't think my parents thought they could have more kids. . . . Wait, I don't even want to think about kids and my parents, because that means . . ."

Talon laughs. "You're not at all how I expected you'd be. In your photos, you look—don't take this the wrong way—like you think you're better than everyone else."

"I hate having my photo taken. I feel really awkward."

"And you're always going to parties."

"My dad's the PM. I get invited to stuff. It's rude to say no to everything."

"I wish we'd met under different circumstances."

"What, like at one of those stupid parties?"

"Hell, no. You wouldn't catch me dead at one of those things. You all look dumb, in your fancy clothes, posing for the cameras."

"You wouldn't have been invited anyway. They have a strict door policy. 'No terrorists allowed.'" In my head, it was funny. We would both laugh. Said out loud, it is anything but. "I'm sorry."

"It's okay. It's what I am. I'm ashamed of what I've done. If I could take it back, I would. I guess Mum isn't the only one who went a little mad after Jez and my dad died."

CHAPTER FOURTEEN

"The exchange will take place over there." Feather points at a patch of green about ten meters or so from where we are standing. I can't see much more of it, because the trees rise up so thickly around us. Several paths wind off from where the four of us are standing by the back of the van, one of which leads to the field. It's a bit less overgrown than the others, but the track the van is parked on is the only one wide enough for a vehicle. It will be hard for Feather and the others to escape if anything goes wrong.

Unsurprisingly I didn't sleep, and my eyes are itchy and sore. My head aches. It was a long drive. We stopped several times, but I wasn't let out. Talon is wearing a mask again, so I guess that means Feather has forgiven him, or at least doesn't want him recognized. I don't think he slept much either; there are dark purple blotches under both his eyes. He hasn't spoken to me or even looked at me since I got out of the van. We're all on edge. Tension crackles in the air like static—a stillness just before something detonates.

Feather reaches into a metal box fastened to the inside wall of the van and pulls out a rifle. She throws it to Scar. "I want you in those trees there. Keep the gun trained on the cops at all times. They'll have their own snipers, so don't use it unless absolutely necessary. But if anyone is going to die, I don't want it to be me."

The thought of Scar watching, gun primed, is not comforting, but then neither is the thought of the police snipers. They might shoot someone accidentally. Involuntarily my gaze flits to Talon.

Feather takes another gun—a small pistol—from the box and tucks it in her belt. "We didn't get you one," she says to Talon. "I know you don't have much experience with guns. Against your ethics."

"And you might get confused and shoot one of us," Scar adds with a leer.

"Right, Princess, listen up." She gives me instructions in short, sharp sentences. I am to walk through the trees and out into the field beyond. I am not to stop. I am not to look back. I must keep walking, no matter what. When I am halfway across the field, the police will release Marble. We will then pass each other. I am not to talk, look, breathe, blink at him. I am to keep walking straight. "Do not mess this up. Talon and I will be behind you the whole time. Any funny business and we will shoot. Got it?"

Whatever happens today, I'll never see Talon again. I

shouldn't care—he's my kidnapper. The man who stole me from my family and kept me locked in darkness and silence and fear. But that is only half the story, and like he said, no one is ever just one thing. It takes a whole lifetime of decisions to make you who you are. As well as Talon the kidnapper, he is Talon the birder, Talon grieving for his dead brother and dad, Talon who was kind to me when no one else was, and . . . and as crazy as it sounds, I like those Talons. I suspect if I spent more time with him, I would like them even more. And now it's time to say good-bye. But how? Words may be a powerful weapon, but sometimes the words you want don't exist.

"Let's get a move on," Feather snaps. She prods me with the gun, and it's too late to say anything to Talon, so I begin walking down the path toward the grassy area. I count my steps in my head to keep me focused. Now is not the time to freak out. It's twenty or so paces to the edge of the field. There is a fence running around it on one side and densely packed trees on the other three. Anyone could be hiding in them.

I'm on my eighteenth step when I hear it: a soft, undulating melody that rises above the sound of our tramping feet.

Talon is whistling. *Twiddle-oo twiddle-eedee.*

A robin.

Twiddle-oo twiddle-eedee.

I turn my head, and he nods so slightly that it is barely a movement at all. *Good-bye, Robyn.*

I nod back. *Good-bye, Talon.*

Sometimes you don't need any words at all.

I break through the trees and start walking across the field. We're on top of a hill, and it's windy. The sky is dark like it might rain any second. The field is small, not much larger than the Downing Street garden. A big chunk of fence is missing where mud and grass have fallen down the hill in a landslide, leaving a steep bank of earth. This quickly levels out into a hill that rolls down into the smudges and smears of trees below. The rest of the field is pretty much empty. Where is Marble? Where are the police? Despite Feather's instructions, I have no clue as to how this is going to work.

I'm more than halfway across the field when a figure emerges from the wood in front of me. He is tall with broad shoulders. A dark-gray hood is pulled up over his head so that I can't see his face, and he is bent over as though in pain. He shuffle-walks like it hurts to move even that tiny amount. Is he sick? Has someone hurt him? Beaten him? I look around for someone else. Surely there's a police officer here? They wouldn't have sent him on his own.

I am right next to him when he collapses. His legs just seem to dissolve underneath him, and he hits the ground with a thump. This is the last thing I was expecting, and I don't know what to do. Feather's scream shakes me to my senses. She and Talon had been hanging back, but she runs out of the trees now. Marble groans, and I turn back to him.

"Are you okay?" I ask. "What happened?"

As I roll him over, his hood falls back to reveal eyes that are blue-gray, not black like his sister's. The rest of his face is covered by a mask. After everything I've been through, my instinct is to run from masked men.

He catches me easily, pulling me down into the cave of his arms. "It's all right, Robyn. My name is Commander Tate. My team and I are here to rescue you. You're safe." As he draws his gun, I feel anything but.

Feather, realizing that this is not her brother, yells, "Shoot! Shoot!" She and Talon run for the trees.

Tate pushes me facedown on the ground at the same time as a black van tears out of the trees and pulls up next to us. A noise like a firework explodes right by my head. Everything is lost in the intense white sound. It is like being at the bottom of a swimming pool. I can see shapes and hear vague noises, but it's all very far away, and then there's a louder rushing noise and I'm spat back out again.

I have heard that sound before. The world has bleached out behind my eyes like the luminous white of newly fallen snow.

My father's blood is a dark stain on the white-laced court-yard. . . . In the distance, the sirens scream, but they are too far away. Already Dad is losing consciousness, his eyes rolling back to milky white, his mouth drooping as the blood spills out. . . .

But it is not my dad's blood this time.

Something wet is dripping down my neck. My fingers come away red and sticky. Tate lets go of me as he clasps his arm to try and stem the blood pouring from it. Figures in black uniforms, their faces covered, pour out of the van. One drops to his knees beside Tate and, after snapping open a first-aid box, begins efficiently bandaging his arm. Another one comes for me. "Robyn, hello. How are you doing?"

"I've . . . I've been better," I say.

The woman pulls her mask up over her face. She smiles. "We're going to get you out of here, okay? Are you hurt?"

I shake my head and she helps me up, one hand under my arm.

The van has blocked my view of the rest of the field, but I can hear that it is chaos out there. Shouts of "Hands up" and "Drop your weapon!" are interspersed with Feather scream-ing for her brother, followed by more gunshots.

"Who is shooting?" I ask, panicked. "I can't see! What's going on?"

"You don't need to worry about that. Hop inside the van for me and let's get you out of here."

"No. You don't understand. Talon—the boy with the green eyes—he isn't like the rest of them. He was kind to me. I have to know if he's all right."

"You shouldn't concern yourself with that." After forcing

me down into the front row of seats, she climbs in after me. "Simon," she calls to the driver, "we're ready."

"You're not listening—"

I'm cut off by the sound of more gunshots and then Talon crying out. This time I move too quickly for her to hold me back. I'm already out of the van and dashing around it before she can even shout. Talon is standing at the edge of the field, right by the landslide. Feather is lying crumpled at his feet. Two officers walk free of the trees behind them with a handcuffed Scar. A third special-ops guy appears a second later. He is lowering a gun. I run across the field, my only thought to get myself between Talon and that gun. Before I can reach him, Talon crouches down. When he stands again, he has Feather's pistol in his hands. What the hell is he doing? The trees will be full of snipers. He should put his hands up. He should surrender.

"Put the gun down, sir," one of the officers says.

I'm close enough now to see that Talon is holding the gun with both hands. They are shaking. His mask and T-shirt are splattered with blood. I say his name and he turns toward the sound of my voice, but his eyes are misty with fear and shock. It almost breaks my heart. One more step, and I am able to clutch his hand, drawing him close to me. "It's okay," I say. "It's all right."

"They—they shot her."

"Yes, but they're not going to shoot you."

"Miss Knollys-Green?" The officer with the gun is very close to us now. Another officer is close behind him, while the third walks Scar back across the field. I'm guessing there must be another van waiting among the trees for any surviving kidnappers.

Surviving kidnappers.

My fingers squeeze Talon's.

"Miss Knollys-Green," the officer says again. "I'm Nigel Thomas. We are here to help you." He is a large man, well over six feet and really muscular, made even more so by his combat gear. Unlike the woman and Tate, he has some sort of glasses over his eyes as well as a mask. He looks like a giant insect or a robot. Not human at all, and not like the kind of man who would understand that not all kidnappers are the same. "It's over, sir," he says to Talon. "One of your gang is injured. The other is in our custody. We have you surrounded. I need you to drop the gun and let Miss Knollys-Green go."

Can't this man see that it's me holding on to him? The gun jerks about in Talon's hand because he is shaking so much.

"He isn't like the others," I say. "He just wanted to help his brother and his friend. You have to promise that you'll listen to him. You won't hurt him." Talon is murmuring incoherently about being fine and that I should just go. I ignore him.

"You have my word that he will be treated fairly. As will the others."

But Talon is not like the others.

I don't want to hand Talon over to these men who don't know him like I do. It's so unfair. The police cheated. None of this would have happened if they'd brought Marble like they'd promised. Why would Dad do this? Why gamble with my life like this?

Not everyone likes the methods I use to run the country.

Your dad may have to make choices . . . difficult ones . . . that we may not agree with or understand. He may not always be able to explain them to us.

Even though I may come first in Dad's heart, I don't always come first in his head. And it is his head that rules Great Britain. I will not send Talon into that world.

For better or worse, we are the choices we make.

Other people's choices have brought us here just as much as Talon's. Feather's. Marble's. Even my dad's.

What can I do, though? I can't fight the police. How can I protect Talon?

Talon and I are pressed up against the edge of the field, right by the gap in the fence I noticed earlier. Below us is the steep drop of the landslide. My father's men stand in front of us with their guns and their masks and their lies. And behind us the land falls away into nothing. Right now, I will happily take nothingness over more death and more lies.

We are the choices we make.

I make mine.

After easing my fingers from Talon's, reassuring him all the time that I'm not going anywhere, it's very easy to press both palms against his chest and push. His eyes widen, and I will him to understand that I'm trying to help him. His arms windmill, and then he is falling. The gun is knocked out of his hand as he hits the ground, and it thankfully bounces away harmlessly.

It isn't a conscious decision that makes me fling myself after him. Instinct takes over, and the next thing I know, my body is hitting the compacted mud and the special-ops men are shouting for me to stop.

CHAPTER FIFTEEN

Falling is rather like flying, except that instead of dropping away below you, the earth hurtles up to smack you in the face again and again. As my head hits a fallen branch, I wonder why I didn't just run. I hadn't had much time to think, and throwing myself down a steep hill seemed the last thing the police would expect me to do and so it would give me the best advantage to get away. Also I'd pushed Talon, so he'd had no choice but rolling; it felt right that I went down the hill the same way. The landslide is steep but short, and after only a couple of turns—legs over head over heels over arms over elbows—I'm at the bottom of it. All my body parts are mixed up, and each one is thundering with pain, and it takes a vital half second before I can stand up. By then, a police officer is already beginning the descent.

"What did you do?" Talon asks, picking himself up and looking at me like I've done something amazing.

There's no time to answer. Instead I grab his arm and tug him into a run. The rest of the hill is less acute, until it flattens out completely and disappears into a bank of trees. "Come on!" I shout, dragging him into the wood.

He is slow at first, but his pace quickens and his eyes have lost their dazed look. I hope that means he didn't bang his head. My own head is oddly empty, like my brain has been shaken out of it.

"You helped me escape," he puffs.

"Just keep running," I say. "They are right behind us."

"Are you sure you want to do this?"

For some reason, the sight of Addy playing on the stairs of Number 10 comes into my mind. It is replaced by the memory of Talon's trembling hand clutching mine. Right now my sister doesn't need me; Talon does. "I'm sure."

And just like that, I go on the run from the British police.

We slam down a makeshift path through the trees. We need to get as far away from the police as we can, and then we need to find somewhere to hide so we can work out what to do next. What the hell are we going to do? I did not think this through. No time for doubt now. "Faster," I say through gritted teeth, storming ahead and forcing Talon to move more quickly to keep up.

It starts to rain. Thin spats at first, and then full-on sheets that soak our clothes instantly and make our hair slick to our heads. Water drips into my eyes, and my feet slide in the mud. The sweat dripping down my back turns icy, and I have a cramp that feels like a knife is sticking right under my ribs. I know the police must be following us, but every time I glance back, I see only rain and leaves. Gray day is turning into gray evening.

There's the sound of snapping undergrowth nearby and I jump, swiveling around in time to see a pebble bounce off the bark of a tree. A blackbird takes off with a hoot and a flap of wings.

"Do you hear that?" Talon whispers.

"It's just a bird."

He shakes his head. At first there is only the sound of the rain hitting the trees, and then I hear it: Something large moves through the undergrowth nearby. There is a squelch of mud followed by a swish of wet leaves. It is getting closer. Talon tugs me down so that we are crouching in the mud behind a bush. We stare out into the gathering darkness.

Squelch swish, squelch squelch—

Talon puts a hand on the small of my back to push me farther down into the undergrowth, just as a police officer, dressed all in black, including a face mask, comes into view. His eyes scan the wood, and my heart thuds in my throat. There are shouts nearby, and a dog barks. The man passes close to our hiding place. Fear turns my stomach over. What am I doing? Where are we going? Do I really think I can outrun the British police, and what for? For a moment I want this to be over, but then I remember: I'm not doing this for me; I'm doing it to protect Talon. I force myself to keep still.

Talon's hand is steady on my back, and I focus on the way his fingers press against the angles of my spine.

Finally the police officer moves away. As he disappears through the trees, Talon and I slowly stand and then run in the opposite direction. The undergrowth is thick, and we keep stumbling over rotten stumps and twisted roots. We're not going fast enough. There are sounds on either side of us, and every now and then I swear I catch a glimpse of a black uniform between the trees. Talon seizes my hand, steering me away from a low-hanging branch that would have knocked me out otherwise. I have to keep focused. I can't afford to let the terror take me over.

"Okay?" Talon asks.

I am about as far from okay as it is possible to be, but I nod. "We need to find somewhere to hide. They'll catch us if we keep running like this."

The trees are dense here, but the undergrowth is low and mostly brambles and nettles. I don't like our chances of hiding among it. We jog on a bit farther. I'm exhausted; this is more running than I've ever done, and the fear is weighing me down too. What will they do when they find us? Handcuff us? Shoot us? Logic tells me they won't shoot the PM's daughter, but my brain is sliding beyond rational thinking now.

Finally I spot somewhere that we could rest awhile. A large bush that looks a bit less prickly than the others. It's surrounded by stinging nettles, but there's no other choice. We pick our way through them as carefully as we can, and then Talon snaps a few branches to create a path for us to crawl through. By some miracle the shrub is wider than it looked at first. There's an open area in the middle of it, laced over with branches and bracken. It's long enough for us to lie down in. We both collapse on our backs, chests heaving. Thanks to the canopy of leaves, the ground is relatively dry and we're protected from the rain.

As we lie there, our breathing slowly evens out, and the wood slides into darkness.

"I left Feather," Talon whispers.

"You didn't have a choice. Someone pushed you down a hill, remember?"

"They shot her."

"She shot them, too."

"She lost it. As soon as she realized that man wasn't Marble. She fired her gun before I could stop her. What will they do to her?"

"I don't know."

"Why did you help me escape?"

I consider lying, but I figure there's already been enough of that, so I answer truthfully. "I didn't want them to hurt you."

"Robyn, I'm your kidnapper."

"I know. Messed up, huh? It just . . . it wasn't fair. They

promised to bring Marble and they didn't. I couldn't let you go to people like that. I didn't think they'd get what you've been through. I was afraid they wouldn't listen to you."

"Do you believe me then, about Jez?"

I picture Michael's red face, his fingers digging into my arms. *You little bitch, you were listening!*

"Michael Bell . . . isn't that *nice*. I mean, he pretends to be, but he has a really nasty temper. I guess I can see how he might lie to protect himself. When I was in Paris in January, just before Dad got shot, I overheard them. They were talking about Jez."

"What did they say?"

I hesitate. "I don't know."

"Robyn?"

"Please stop pushing me. I just . . . Well, Michael said something about a journalist sniffing around an incident that happened a couple of years back. He told my dad that he was up to his neck in it too—whatever it was. Then . . . in the hospital, after the shooting, Dad told me the kid who died was called Jeremy Fletcher."

"Right. Well, that says it all then."

"He said it was an accident! He said it wasn't Michael's fault. My dad had just been shot. You have no idea what it was like that day. I'd been so angry with Dad because I thought he was hiding something, and then he got shot. And I thought he was going to die, and that would be it. He'd die thinking I was mad at him." Now that I've started talking, I can't stop. "And then when he didn't die, I just wanted everything to be all right. To go back to the way it was. He told me it was all right, that nothing bad had happened. I just . . . I wanted to believe him. I'm sorry about your brother. I am, really." I sniff.

"Hey, hey. It's okay. Shh. It's okay. I can't believe you helped me escape and then came with me. You could be home by now."

"But then I wouldn't be with you." I turn away, embarrassed because I am sweaty and bloodstained and my hair is a cropped mess.

He tilts my chin toward him, and I see none of that matters. He doesn't care what I look like or who I am or where I came from. He just cares about me. "Robyn Knollys-Green," he whispers, "you are the bravest person I've ever met."

"Am I?"

"Yeah." He smiles. "And possibly the stupidest. You pushed me down a freaking hill. I could have broken my neck."

"But you didn't."

His smile fades, and I sense mine does too.

"What are we going to do?" I ask.

"Rest up here for a while. Sleep maybe?"

"I meant tomorrow. We can't run forever."

"No."

An owl sounds in the trees above us. It is long and mournful like a wail.

"There's a guy I know. He used to work for Bell-Barkov and got us some information on them. Feather freaked him out, though, and he refused to help us any more. But him and me got on okay. He was sad about what happened to Jez. He might let me stay with him for a while. A few days, anyway."

"Will he mind you bringing along a hostage?"

"You pushed me, remember? Technically, doesn't that make me your hostage?"

"What about your mum? Wouldn't she help?"

"No. She's not well. I wouldn't want to get her involved."

"He'll probably recognize me, this friend of yours. People sometimes do. I should go home anyway. I'll see you settled with this guy and then I'll turn myself in."

"You haven't done anything wrong. They won't be cross with you."

"I helped a terrorist escape. That might be a little hard to explain. I'll speak to my dad about Jez. I'll try to ask Michael what happened. I'll get them to do something about it. I don't know what or how, but I will."

"Thank you."

We fall into a comfortable silence. We don't hear any shouts or dogs, and even the rain has stopped. "I hope Feather's all right," Talon says after a while.

"Why do you care so much about her?"

"I know it's hard to understand, but she was there for me when no one else was."

"She got you involved in a kidnapping. She nearly got you shot!"

"It was my choice to kidnap you. She didn't make me."

The leaves over our hiding place are edged in silver from the moon, and I run my finger along one, tracing the light. The moonlight splashes on the back of my hand, like a stain. Our breathing is even now, his an echo of mine. "Why are you called Talon?"

"Feather and Marble had nicknames, and I wanted one too. I thought it sounded cool at the time. Feather's is because of her hair. She has a white patch just here and it looks like, well, a feather."

"And Marble's?"

"Because he liked playing marbles as a kid."

"Seriously? Ha! You said when we first met that you were named for the earth."

"I can be a pretentious dick sometimes. You know, we should probably try to get some sleep."

"Yeah."

His breath hitches as I run my fingers down his wrist and the tiny bones of his hand. I scoop up his fingers, entwining them with mine. This is crazy, but I don't care. Who knows what will happen tomorrow? This might be the last time we're ever together.

"Would it be weird to say I'll miss you?"

"Yes, but I'll miss you, too." He squeezes my hand before releasing it. "Robyn, I like you a lot. But that's so messed up. I'm already in enough trouble. And I—I don't see how anything good can come of this. Tomorrow I'll be gone and you'll be home."

"I could come with you, to your friend's." It's a stupid suggestion, though.

"That's not a good idea. But I do like you."

"I like you, too." I reach for his hand again. "This is okay, though, right? I mean, if you think so."

His fingers close around mine. "Yeah, I think so."

I wake up, freezing; my whole body is shaking. A murky gray light glimmers through the overhanging branches, catching the thin layer of frost on all the leaves. A squirrel is sniffing around in the undergrowth on the other side of the small clearing beyond the bush we are hidden in. It looks up suddenly, a nut caught between its claws, its small black nose twitching.

Talon is asleep next to me, his hand still in mine. I slip my fingers free and notice that a mobile phone has slid out from his trouser pocket and is lying on the ground between us. Why didn't he mention it last night? He could have called his friend. Maybe like me he wanted one more night together.

Should I call Dad? I could explain about Talon, and then

he could intervene with the police: make them understand that Talon is not like Scar and Feather. Before I can change my mind, I pick the phone up and then carefully crawl back through the trees. After a furtive glance around to make sure there are no police nearby, I stand up and head through the trees a bit. For some reason I don't want Talon to overhear me. Is that because I know what I'm doing is stupid? I don't care. I'm going to do it anyway. I'm still clinging to the thin hope that Dad didn't know the full extent of what Michael had done. If I can make him understand, then maybe he'll help Talon.

I dial Dad's mobile number with shaking fingers. It rings, once, twice, three times, and then he is there, sounding as though he is standing right next to me. I try to keep my breath even, but it is loud, like the rush of a train.

"Hello, Knollys-Green speaking," Dad says.

I don't reply.

"Hello?"

I breathe out, breathe in, but I don't speak.

"Robyn? Is that you? Where the hell are you? What's going on? The police said you ran away." He is furious, and I'm suddenly back in that hotel suite in Paris. *You're up to your neck in this, Stephen, just like me.*

Dad has always known the truth about Jez, and he did nothing.

The phone slides from my hand and bounces a couple of

times on the grass. It comes to rest at Talon's feet. He stoops to pick it up. "Who did you ring?"

"No one. It doesn't matter."

The coldness in his eyes turns the blood in my veins to ice. He knows I called Dad.

"I just wanted to speak to him. I was hoping he'd help you. I thought if he only understood . . ." I trail off and then add pathetically, "He's my dad." Like that explains everything, but I guess in a way it does. The British prime minister is my father, and the guy in front of me is my kidnapper.

Then there's a shout from behind us, followed by the howls of dogs.

"You told your dad where we were?"

"No! How could I? I don't even know where we are! Please, listen—"

But it's already too late. Men and dogs spill out from the trees all around us. There is snarling and shouting, and none of that is as scary as the look of betrayal in Talon's eyes. "Talon . . ."

The dogs bark and tug on their leads, their jaws a slobbering mass of teeth and gums. Then Commander Thomas shoves his way through the fray. Without any warning, he lifts his rifle and brings the butt down on the back of Talon's head. Talon drops like a stone.

And something inside me detonates. Because I am sick of lies and misunderstandings and violence and people making decisions for me. I throw myself at Thomas, and I am fingernails scratching and fists pummeling and feet kicking. But none of it is enough. I am not enough. Other hands slide around my waist and tug me easily away. They hold me tightly, even as I scream so loudly that it tears the world apart. Talon is motionless at my feet. His eyes are closed, and blood trickles from the gash to his skull, and I wonder if I'm doomed to watch everyone I love lie face-down in their own blood.

CHAPTER SIXTEEN

Dr. Flight's smile is as sweet as treacle; just looking at it is enough to rot your teeth. "Breathe in for me," she says. The stethoscope is cold against my skin. After giving me a rehydration solution, she looked at my injuries—most of them are healing now—but she spent a long time examining my finger. She seemed satisfied and just reapplied a bandage. She gives me a tetanus shot and then says, "I'm sorry for the way you've been treated so far, but we just need to be very clear that you pose no threat."

I am dressed in a blue tracksuit. Beneath it I'm a thin slab of white meat. My chest juts out like a cliff over the inlet of my belly, coming to knotty peaks at my collarbone.

Talon had begun to come around while I was still fighting the police, but he was obviously in a bad way. The police handcuffed both of us and then walked us to separate vans. Then three police officers, including the one called Thomas, had accompanied me on the long journey here, a near–surgically clean white box in a vast building that is surrounded on all sides by high, barbed fences. From the outside, the place looked decayed, like one strong gust of wind could blow it away. The tangle of wires and assorted satellite dishes on its roof looked like legs. They jerked in the strong breeze, like the whole thing was trying to scuttle back into the hill behind it: an insect crawling into its hole. As we got closer, and the wind picked up even more, the building's legs seemed to go into spasm to the accompaniment of clanging metal that screeched like cicadas.

When we drew up outside, a special-forces agent tugged me roughly from the car, still handcuffed, and walked me down various corridors to this room. Dr. Flight was indignant when she saw me and demanded that they take the cuffs off *at once*.

I haven't seen Talon since the woods, and no one will answer any of my questions about him or anything else.

Am I a patient here or a prisoner?

"Can I go home now?" I ask as the doctor tidies up her tray of equipment.

She dumps the used syringe in the bin, pulls off the surgical gloves, and then starts wrapping up the remaining gauze before answering. "Not just yet."

"When, then?"

"Well, really, that depends on you." She secures the end of the gauze with a safety pin. "We want to help you, Robyn, but you have to help us, too." She smiles her treacle smile again. "The officers here are sworn to protect the country." Her voice is like honey.

"I'm not dangerous."

"No, of course you're not." She pats my knee. "Now you are all patched up on the outside. How about getting you patched up on the inside? A nice plate of scrambled eggs on toast, eh? Sound good?"

My stomach betrays me by gurgling loudly.

There's a knock on the door, and Commander Thomas sticks his head in. "Okay to have a little chat with Robyn now?"

The doctor gives a smile as sweet as cotton candy and gestures him in.

"How are you holding up, Miss Knollys-Green?" he asks, settling into a chair.

"Where's Talon?"

"Do you mean Samuel Fletcher? He is in a secure unit. He can't hurt you again."

"He didn't hurt me. He was kind. Feather and Scar are the ones behind all this. They made him take me." My head is hurting, like a percussion orchestra is playing inside it, and the sound of my blood is the drum. I haven't eaten anything since yesterday morning, and I'm sick and dizzy. The lights are bright in here, and yet the room seems full of moving shadow. Dark, undulating shapes rise up at the corner of my eyes and creep toward me like oil slicks. I rub my eyes to clear my vision.

The police officer has to repeat what he's just said. "You like this Samuel. Is that why you helped him escape yesterday? Or did he force you?"

"It was a very dangerous thing to do, Robyn," the doctor says.

"He didn't make me do anything. You broke your promise. You didn't free Marble."

"Marble is a known terrorist. He is charged with shooting your father," says Thomas.

"But that isn't Talon's fault. You're getting this all wrong. Talon only kidnapped me because the police wouldn't listen to him when he said that Michael Bell had killed his brother."

"Michael Bell? Sorry, who are you talking about?"

"Michael Bell—the head of Bell-Barkov. My godfather. Dad's best friend. There's this drug, and it isn't safe. Michael knew it wasn't, but he still let it be used on kids, and Talon's brother died."

"Samuel told you that Michael Bell killed his brother and that's why you helped him to escape?"

"Yes. No. It wasn't as simple as that. You're not listening. I knew you wouldn't; that's why we ran yesterday. I—I didn't want you to hurt Talon. He was kind to me. He— He—" *You told your dad where we were.*

"Robyn, I want you to understand that what these people did, including this Talon, was wrong. They are all going to face charges of kidnapping, unlawful imprisonment, and terrorism. They will be going to prison for a long time."

"No! Not Talon. It's not fair."

"There is a condition, you know," the doctor says in her honeyed tone. "It's called Stockholm syndrome. It is where someone who has been in captivity begins to have sympathy for her captor. Sometimes even feelings of love develop."

"I do not have that! You definitely do not understand."

The officer is looking at me as if I'm insane, and I realize it is pointless. Even my own father lied to me about this. I stand up. "I want to go home now."

"Of course you do, and you can very soon, but first we just need to understand what happened yesterday. And we'd like to have someone talk to you about your time in captivity."

"I don't want to talk anymore. I want to go home, but first . . . I want to see Talon."

"I'm afraid that won't be possible."

"Why not? What have you done with him?"

"It's not a case of that. We assure you that he is quite all right. He is in the holding cells—"

"I want to see him NOW." I fling Dr. Flight's tray across the room, narrowly missing Thomas's head. The doctor's smile drips from her face like melted chocolate. "Robyn, you need to calm down," she urges.

But I'm tired of being calm, and I'm fed up with doing what I'm told.

I walk to the door, sidestepping Thomas's attempts to stop me.

"Robyn, for goodness' sake," the doctor says. "Where are you going?"

"We can sort this out," Thomas says.

Maybe they can, but it won't be in the way I want, so I start to run. I am still dizzy, but adrenaline has kicked in, and I move fast. So does Thomas. He snatches for me, but I spin away and open the door at the end of the hall. I dash through the gap and then pull the door shut behind me. After grabbing a nearby chair, I ram it under the door handle. It won't hold for long, but maybe it will give me enough time to find Talon.

I run on through six more doors, taking as many corners as I can to try to throw Thomas off my scent. Then I come out into a wide atrium. I take in the scene quickly. There's a circular reception desk, and in front of it are three long rows of chairs. To the left and right of the desk are doors, and behind the chairs, an ornate red rug leads like a tongue to a set of glass doors that open out onto a tarmacked forecourt. Sunshine glints on the glass, making the doors shine.

I turn back to the desk. I'm not leaving here without seeing Talon. Thomas mentioned that he was in a holding cell. There must be a map somewhere. I pull open a couple of the drawers in the desk. I doubt very much that any map I find is going to say *Terrorists stored here*, but at least it might give me some indication as to where I am now and in which direction I should head first.

The double doors slide open as I am searching the third drawer. Two men enter. I duck behind the desk and then crawl on my hands and knees until I can peer around it to watch them. Thankfully they don't hesitate but head straight for the door I just ran through. "Distress signal came from down here," one says. The other man nods, and the two of them disappear through the door.

I count to twenty, to make sure they aren't coming back, and then stand slowly and resume my search of the desk. The third drawer contains only pens, paper, and endless appointment diaries. The sound of footsteps coming from the web of corridors reminds me that I need to hurry up. I shove everything back into the drawer, and my fingers run over something smooth at the bottom. A piece of paper has been taped there. It is a map of fire exits.

One corner rips as I tear it out of the drawer. I lay it on the desk, pushing back the curling corners. The building is immense, and the map is complicated. There are so many different wings. Corridors lead to more corridors. Panic is beginning to set in. I will never find Talon in this place. And then finally I spot the words "holding area." They have been handwritten in fading blue pen on a large gray box that looks like some sort of basement or cellar. A holding area could hold anything, but I have a feeling that what it contains at the moment are Talon, Feather, and Scar. Besides, it's the only clue I have, and I'm not prepared to admit defeat yet.

According to the map, there should be a lift down to the basement at the end of one of the hallways off the reception area. A woman in uniform appears through a door to the right of me just as I am deciding which corridor to take. Her cry of "Hey! Stop!" leaves me no time for any extended decision making. To the sound of her stamping feet chasing me, I flee down a hall that I hope will lead to the lift and Talon.

The corridor bends sharply to the right, and I risk a glance back as I make the turn. A man in uniform has joined the woman, and the two are gaining on me fast. I force myself to run harder, nearly smashing into the wall as I skid on the shiny floor. The corridor branches out, to become two forks. I make a snap decision and take the left corridor and immediately regret it when I see that it leads to a set of double doors that are most definitely not a lift. My hands are shaking so much that I can't get a proper grip on the door. "Wait!" The woman lunges for me just as I manage to turn the handle.

I dance away, spinning out of her hands, and fly through the open door. The officers are right behind me. As I kick the doors shut, there is the howl of fingers caught. They pull free, and I'm able to shut the double doors. If I can just secure them somehow, I will have a chance. There is nothing, though. . . . No rod, no . . . Wait. Bolts. Four of them, two on each door, one that can be driven into the ceiling and

another for the floor on each side. I slam the top two home.
My breathing eases as I secure the bottom two. The bolts are
strong, but so are the police; four bolts won't keep them out
for long, but a single second is a bonus now.

I hurry down the stairs behind me. The corridor beyond
is empty, so I creep out and jog to the end of the hall. To the
right is the lift. It is an old service one, with cagelike doors. I
race to it and press the call button; there's a screech of metal
as it descends.

I take the lift down to the basement. It comes to a stop,
and I slide the gates open to reveal a large room, its bare concrete walls illuminated by fluorescent strip lighting. Racks
of shelves fill the enormous space. They run for what seems
like miles in all directions. Each shelf is crammed with con-
tainers, as well as what look like piles of syringes, all sealed
in plastic, scalpels, and other medical equipment. There is
a single metal door opposite the lift. A rusted sign above it
reads TO THE HOLDING AREA.

After getting out of the lift, I leave the door open, partly
because I don't have the strength to do anything else and
partly because I have some notion that these sorts of lifts can't
be called to other floors if their doors aren't closed.

People are always talking about a sixth sense. That feeling you get, when you just know. I just *know* as soon as I
enter the dark, grim corridor beyond the door marked TO THE
HOLDING AREA that I am going to find Talon at the end of it.

Rotting cardboard boxes, old filing cabinets, and other junk block my path, as if someone is keen to make you think that this is a disused corridor. It leads to nothing, so best just turn around and go back the way you've come. I don't turn back. I stalk through the darkness, swearing and yelping as my body bashes into the debris piled up here.

Eventually, the hallway widens. I take another step forward, and a row of strip lights flashes on above me. The space is wider here, brighter, cleaner. In the middle of this area is a bank of desks. Blinking computers sit among piles of paper. I come upon what looks like a small galley kitchen. A female police officer is in it, humming to herself and making a cup of tea. Very quietly, I shut the door and prop one of the chairs under the handle to keep it closed. I hear a muffled female voice say, "What the hell?" followed by banging. At the end of the hall, to the left, I discover the cells, little more than crevices carved out of the walls, with iron bars running across each one.

The first two are empty. In the third, I find a shirtless Scar doing push-ups. I recognize him instantly, even though I have never seen him without his mask. The stitches on a couple of his fingers have burst, and blood congeals on the concrete beneath him. "Knew you couldn't live without me, Princess," he says, without looking up. If he's surprised to see me here, he doesn't show it. After grinding out another push-up, he stands up. "Miss me?" he asks.

"Good-bye, Scar," I say, walking away. It is Talon I have come for. Scar can rot down here, for all I care.

I find Talon, three cells down, and the sight of him stops my heart. He is lying on a cot, staring up at the ceiling. There is blood on his collar, presumably from the knock to the back of his head, and a bruise on his cheekbone. He rolls out of the bed slowly when he spots me. I open my mouth to speak. No words come. His hands slide over mine as I grip the bars, and for a while I have no idea if I am holding him up or he is holding me.

"I'm sorr—," I begin.

"You came for me," he interrupts.

I grasp his fingers tighter. "I'll always come for you."

His eyes are bloodshot; the green light in them dimmed, almost gone.

"Let's get you out of here." As I say the words, I realize I mean it. I didn't come to say good-bye. I came to set him free, because the police won't believe him and he'll never get justice for his brother if he stays locked up. "I've got a map. We can find a secret way out."

"You shouldn't get yourself into trouble for me. I deserve this, Robyn. I need to be punished for what I did."

There's a sound of splintering wood from farther up the corridor. "We don't have long," I say.

"Will you do me a favor and just see if Feather is all right?"

"You're kidding me."

"Please, Robyn. I know what she's done, but she was in a bad way and—and she was my friend once. And she's Marble's sister. I owe it to him."

Feather is on the floor of the next cell, her back against the wall. Her eyes are closed, the lids heavy and dark, and there's a bandage around one of her arms. It's the first time I've seen her without the mask. What I notice first is the white patch of hair on her head. It looks like feathers, just as Talon said it did.

I hate this woman. She took me from my family because she wanted to get her brother back, and she never thought, not once, about what the kidnapping would do to me. Because of her, I have learned that everything I believed is wrong, and I have no idea how to begin again with what I have. I step away from her cell. Who cares if she lives or dies? She wouldn't care if it was the other way around. Still, I draw a deep breath, already knowing that I can't just walk away.

"Talon wants to know if you're okay."

"Been better." She struggles to stand up, grimacing in pain. "Little Bird is out of her cage, then."

"And Little Bitch is in hers, where she belongs."

"Grown claws then since I last saw you, or should I call them talons." Her laugh becomes a hacking cough that racks her whole body. "Is this a rescue mission? If he tells you to save me, don't bother. I'd rather die than be saved by you."

"Good," I reply. I'm about to walk away when she says, "It

was me, you know. I shot your father. I wish I'd killed him. He is just as guilty as Michael Bell."

My hands are trembling with anger. I march back down the corridor to the desks. None of the cells have locks, and that means the doors must be controlled centrally somehow. I wiggle the mouse of one of the computers, and the screen lights up and asks me to enter a password. I don't even bother trying to guess. I open a few of the drawers in the desk beneath it. Most of the drawers are empty, apart from the usual stationery supplies. Then I rummage around on the next desk, after which I bend down to peer under it. No secrets there, just smooth wood. I check the other desks, and on the fourth one, I find it: a control panel, with red dots and beside them buttons, matching the layout of the cells behind me. I press one. There's a whirl and a click and then the bars on Feather's cell slide down.

I bunch my hands into fists.

"Robyn," Talon calls as I stalk past his cell. "Don't! She isn't worth it."

Feather comes out smiling. "All right, Princess."

I punch her in the face, my knuckles connecting with her jaw. Her head slams back against the bars of her cell, and blood sprays out. She laughs. "That all you got?"

She may be small, but she's fast. Her hands come up and seize my throat, pushing me into the wall behind me. No matter how hard I bat at her arms and face, she doesn't let go. Her hands tighten around my neck. This is it: This is how I'm going to die. A thousand memories swim in my head. *Addy, Dad, Mum . . . Talon's hand in mine.*

The inside of my lids is red and warm like a fire. I leap into its brightness. It wraps itself around me, like a warm hand. *I am lying under the bush in the wood. Nearby, a bird cries to its mate as it builds a nest.*

Talon smiles down at me. "Hello, you. Did you miss me?"

I. Am. Not. Ready. To *die*. With my last ounce of strength, I kick her hard in the shin. She gasps in pain, and I head-butt her. My forehead smashes against her nose. Her hands fly to her face, and I gasp air. Feather recovers quickly and starts to slap me around the head. I collapse under her blows, and she takes the opportunity to run down the corridor. She's opened the doors to all the cells before I'm on my feet.

Talon comes out first. Scar is right behind him. He stretches, a carnal grin spreading across his face as he walks slowly toward me. Talon goes to punch him, but Scar knocks him to the ground. He kicks him in the gut, in the chest, and finally in the head. Talon lies still. From down the corridor, Feather laughs.

No!

I have no weapon and Scar is at least twice my size, but I fling myself at him anyway, fists flying and legs kicking. He swipes me away as easily as if I were a fly. I land heavily against the bars of one of the cells, winding myself. Scar crouches over me, catching my hands and holding them above my head. I scream as he begins to run his hands over me, but he is just looking for the map. He pulls it free of my back pocket and stands up. "Be seeing you, Princess." He walks over to Feather, who grins and takes the map from him.

What have I done? By coming here, I have helped two violent criminals escape and got Talon badly hurt.

I try to stand, but my legs have forgotten what they are for. All I can do is watch as Feather and Scar head for the exit. Then there is a sound of cracking, and the policewoman finally breaks out of the kitchen. "Stop right there," she yells at Scar and Feather.

"Chill out, lady," Scar says. "There's no problem here."

"I'll be the judge of that." The police officer is at the bank of computers now, and she picks up a radio. "This is the holding area. Request immediate assis—"

Feather hits her once on the side of the head and then again and again until the woman falls to the floor. *Move, Robyn. Move.* It is as much as I can do to crawl over to Talon; my fingers snag in his hair. I close my eyes, trying to gather my strength.

I open them again as I hear shouting. Six figures in black gear pour in to surround Feather and Scar. There are more yells: "Hands up or we will shoot!" Then comes the rapid fire of a gun, followed by a whooshing noise, and the room begins to fill up with smoke.

There are human shapes in the haze. Someone bends over me. I hear the snicker-suck of breath through a mask. Something is passed over my head and secured. My eyes clear, as do my lungs, and I can breathe again.

Then Talon is dragged away from me. I scream into the mask and lash out. The masked figure falls back, startled. I get my arms more securely around Talon and pull him up into my lap, clamping my arms and legs around him. No one is taking him away from me. Not this time. I brush his hair back gently from his face. The fog—tear gas, I guess—is still filling up the room. After taking a deep gulp of air, I take the mask off and put it over Talon's face. *Breathe, Talon. Breathe. Breathe.*

I hold on for as long as I can, but finally I have to take a breath. The gas immediately fills my lungs again. I keep stroking Talon's hair. A man is walking toward me. There is something shiny on his feet. Something polished. Shoes. He crouches before me and murmurs something. I lean forward. What? My name. He is saying my name.

As my last wisp of oxygen is swallowed up by the gas, I look up into his face. My own eyes stare back at me. Eyes that are sometimes brown and sometimes green and sometimes gold.

"Dad," I whisper. *"Dad."*

CHAPTER SEVENTEEN

I wake up tucked under a duvet in a long, narrow room. Late-afternoon sunshine pours through a large window to the left, its panels making lines like the bars of a cage across the bed. Dad is seated beside me, a newspaper in his hands. He folds it when he sees I'm awake. "You slept for a long time. How do you feel?"

Like I've been microwaved.

"Water," I gasp.

He guides the straw from a plastic beaker to my mouth. "They released tear gas into the cells yesterday. We had no idea you were in there. Idiots. The whole thing was badly bungled." He replaces the cup on the bedside table. "We've missed you so much. You have no idea—"

"Where's Mum?"

"At home. I wanted to make sure you were in an acceptable state before she saw you. She's been very worried. We both have. . . . And your hair. Oh, Robyn, what have they done to you . . . ?" He trails off. "Can I get you something? More water? Something to eat?"

I shake my head and gingerly push myself up to a sitting position. My body is made of porcelain; the smallest bump and I'll shatter.

"Careful, careful," Dad says, trying to help me, until I put my hand up for him to back off. He sits back down in the chair. "You are rather bashed up. It is going to take a long time for all of this to heal." He isn't just talking about my bruises.

I want more water, but this time I reach for it myself and take a long, long gulp. My head is clearing, and with the warm sun on my face, I start to feel less like something that belongs in a rubbish bin.

"Where am I? They wouldn't tell me."

"I'm sorry about that. When you ran during the rescue on Saturday afternoon, it confused everything. There was some panic and some ludicrous notion that you might have become a terrorist." He gives a humorless snort. I don't even smile. "You're in a detention center. You've been here since yesterday."

Everything comes back to me in a rush. Talon in that cell. Scar. The police officers bursting in. And the gas.

The clock on the wall ticks through the seconds. Dad is looking at me, his hands steepled like he's praying.

"You lied to me. In Paris, after the shooting, you said that Jez—Jeremy Fletcher wasn't killed by Michael's drug. That wasn't true, was it?"

"No." His sigh seems to hold the whole world.

"You promised me." But I'm not talking about Jez anymore. "You promised after you got shot that everything was okay. You said nothing bad would ever happen again, but it did. They took me, and you didn't do anything to stop it. Ten days I was there. *Ten days*, and where were you?"

"I did everything I could. Robyn, darling, please," he says, reaching toward me.

I shove his hands away. "Not enough."

"I can explain. Everything. Truthfully this time."

"I don't believe you. All you do is lie." I push the duvet cover off and stand up. "I want to go home. I want my mum and my sister. You don't give a shit about me."

"I do. I do. Robyn, calm down, please. You need to rest."

"I've been so scared. You don't know what they *did*." My voice breaks and my shoulders heave as the tears come, and my legs give way beneath me. I fall back against the bed. He sits down beside me. He smells of aftershave and brandy and the cigars that he isn't supposed to smoke.

"Will you let me explain? Will you listen to me?" he asks.

"I should have trusted you with the truth in January," Dad says. We are sitting—I'm wrapped in about three hundred blankets—in a miniature courtyard somewhere in the bowels of the building. It is surrounded on all sides by high brick walls with a green gate.

Dad hadn't wanted to come outside. He'd been worried I wasn't up to it, but I have been stuck inside for too long. I want to feel the sun on my face and have the air ruffle my short hair. Sunshine breaks through the heavy cloud, making everything golden. Talon would love it here. Suddenly I am back in that smoke-filled room, coughing and spluttering on the gas and fighting with everything I have to hang on to Talon. I wasn't strong enough. They took him away again, and I haven't seen him since.

Beside me, Dad draws a long, deep breath. "It's peaceful, isn't it? When all this is over, I'd like to build a garden just like this one."

I sense him trying to catch my eye, but I stare resolutely ahead. I agreed to listen to him. I didn't agree to believe him, or to speak to him.

Dad starts to talk. "The day you were born was one of the best of my life. You were a tiny, scrunched-up creature, lying on your mother's chest as she slept. I picked you up and I took you over to the window and I held you up so you could see out across the city. And you smiled. People have told me a hundred times since that newborns can't smile. I don't care. They weren't there. It was only you and me, and you smiled at me."

I break my silence. "Dad, did Michael know that the drug Jeremy Fletcher took was dangerous?"

"The regulatory authority had granted approval for it to

be used on patients. We're talking about a tragic death—"

I sigh. Dad is still trying to spin the truth. "Did Michael know that there was a problem with the drug or not? Dad, come on. You promised the truth this time."

He rubs his temples. "Yes. As I understand it, Bell-Barkov took some shortcuts during earlier testing phases."

"To save money."

"To expedite the drug's release on the market. Some side effects of Amabim-F emerged with trial patients, but only when the drug was given at higher dosages. Swelling and the like. A monkey had also died, apparently, but who knows if that was related?"

"But a guy died too," I say, remembering what Talon told me.

"Did he? I don't know about that."

"So what happened about Jez, I mean Jeremy?"

"Michael left the voice mail I told you about in Paris very early one morning, and it was a while before I was able to call him back. When I did get hold of him, he was hysterical. He said that the situation was much worse than first suspected. The company commissioned to carry out the drug trial on the boy had reported inadequate staffing levels. The consultant on duty had called in sick the previous night, leaving only a skeletal and inexperienced staff to carry out the trial. It should have been canceled the moment the senior doctor was unable to attend, but it wasn't."

"What are you saying? I don't understand."

"There is a very real possibility that if the proper medical care had been given, the boy might not have died. This company, Glindeson, was solely to blame on that front."

"He has a name, you know," I say. "He is not just 'the boy.'"

"You are very angry, Robyn."

"I have every right to be. I was kidnapped because of what you did."

"The AFC are terrorists. There is no justification for what they've done."

Talon wasn't a terrorist. He was just desperate to be heard.

Dad is still talking. "Michael genuinely believed that these little issues had been resolved. They had delayed stage two of the clinical trials, where patients with the disease are treated, for more than six months while they worked to identify what was causing these adverse reactions. 'They were fixed,' Michael kept saying. 'I swear to you, Stephen, that they were all fixed. We haven't had a single problem with the drug since then.'"

Until Jez.

"With one thing and another, I didn't speak to Michael for the rest of that day," Dad continues. "When I called the following morning, he was chirpier. It now seemed likely that the child"—he catches my eye and corrects himself—"that *Jeremy* died of some underlying health issues. Michael said he'd found a pathologist willing to write a report clearing Amabim-F. The words 'willing to' should have rung alarm bells, but they didn't. I was busy, and I'd heard what I wanted: Michael's company wasn't to blame. I didn't ask any questions. I told him it was great news, and I moved on with my day."

Dad pauses. The garden is very still. The only sound is a bird building a nest in the tree beside us and occasionally tweeting at its mate.

"I have gone over that conversation in my mind so very many times in the last week or so. If only I had listened more carefully! 'How easy it is to judge rightly after one sees what evil comes from judging wrongly.' I swear to you on my life and all the lives I hold even dearer to me, I did not know that Michael's drug caused that boy's death."

Do I believe him? I don't know.

"So when did you find out?" I ask.

"A few weeks after the fire at Bell-Barkov last October. You may remember that your mother and I went up to stay with the Bells. We wanted to show our support for them. Michael behaved very strangely the whole time. He was drinking heavily and was clearly very agitated about something. Finally, on the Sunday, over a round of golf, I got it out of him. He confessed that the problems with Amabim-F had not been fixed prior to Jeremy's death. He also told me that he had paid someone to set fire to the company headquarters."

"*What?*"

"Yes, it's true. He'd grown increasingly paranoid. The boy's father was sending letters, a journalist was onto him, and the AFC were issuing death threats. 'There was evidence,' he kept saying. 'I didn't want them to find it.' He didn't specify who *they* were."

"You knew all of this and you said *nothing?*"

"Michael is my oldest friend."

"He set fire to his own offices. He killed a kid. There was clearly something wrong with him!"

"It isn't as simple as that. I ordered him to come clean. I threatened to report it myself. But he was crying and begging and even threatening to hurt himself. It—it scared me. I have known Michael nearly all my life. He's been there for me so many times, and now he needed me. I agreed to give him some time. A few days at first, and then I agreed to a week. Then the week became a month became two. For the first time in my life, I was paralyzed, unable to make a decision."

I clutch the blankets more firmly around my shoulders. I can't believe what I'm hearing.

"I told myself the drug was a good one. It would save so many people with kidney failure. Maybe that child's death *had* been unrelated. And besides, Michael was my friend, my oldest and closest friend. I owe him so much. Could I really destroy him like this? And what about me? Questions would surely be asked. How much did I know? Why had I waited so long to tell the truth?"

"So you were just thinking of yourself."

"And you and your mother and Addy. Can you imagine the scandal if it had come out?"

"Did Michael pay you to keep quiet?"

"No! I did this out of friendship, not for money." He is indignant.

"But Michael has lent you money. You told me about it in Paris."

"That was a loan." He draws a deep breath. "I didn't lie to you about that. But yes, I was aware that it would look bad if anyone found out I knew about that child's death."

"It would look like a bribe."

He nods. "I was nearly mad with worry, and so the only sensible thing seemed to be to put the whole sorry problem out of my head. This was in December of last year. It was nearly Christmas. I decided to give myself the festive season to think it all over, and I would make a final decision in the new year. Then we went to Paris, and Michael told me about the letter from the journalist. I knew then that I couldn't tell the truth; it was too late. Too much was at stake, so I kept quiet. And after the shooting, I felt justified. These people were killers. I was trying to protect you when I lied, Robyn. You and Michael."

And yourself.

"I almost don't care that you lied to me," I say. "I care more that you didn't tell anyone the truth. Jeremy's brother was one of my kidnappers. Did you know that?"

"He was a very sick little boy. He would have died anyway. And his parents knew of the risks involved in a clinical trial."

"So it's their fault?" I stand up angrily, my chrysalis of blankets falling to the ground. "How can you say that?"

Dad picks up the blankets and tries to wrap them around me again, but I yank them away from him. He collapses back on the bench and drops his head into his hands.

"You're still trying to spin it. To make yourself look better."

"I know." He stares up at me, and for once his eyes are just one shade. No sprinkling of gold, no flecks of green—just large brown disks that glisten in the light. Is my dad crying? It surprises me so much that I sit back down again.

"I have paid for my part in this. Losing you. That second video, when that woman cut your finger. I can't . . . And then it slowly dawned on me that it was all connected—that you were suffering because of me. It has been . . . well . . . no hell could be worse."

"When did you accept that my kidnapping wasn't just about freeing Kyle Jefferies?"

"The police spoke to him on the day you were taken. It took a while, but when he learned the full extent of his sister's plans, he withdrew his original statement. He said he wasn't to blame for shooting me. It had been his sister, Feather. For some reason, he'd been protecting her. Eventually the whole story of his sister's vendetta against Bell-Barkov emerged. He said he suspected that she wasn't working alone. There was a man who lived with them, he said, whose brother had died after taking Amabim-F."

"What's going to happen now?" I draw my knees up so I can rest my head on them. The sun is brighter and the garden smells of sunshine. There was a time when I didn't think I'd ever see the sun again, didn't think I'd ever see anything except for four white walls and a tiny slice of sky through a high-up window.

"What do you mean?"

"Will you tell everyone about Michael and the drug and how you kept quiet about it all?"

"I already have. There'll be an investigation and probably a trial. Bell-Barkov will be investigated, as will Michael and Glindeson, the company that oversaw the drug trial Jez was involved in. Criminal charges will probably be brought against Michael for the fire, but the police will want to establish how many other people were involved first. There'll also be an inquiry into Jeremy's death. His parents will finally have justice."

"Talon's dad is dead. He—he killed himself."

"I am very sorry to hear that. Another tragedy that could have prevented had I acted sooner. He was kind to you, was he, this Talon, while you were in captivity?"

"Yes. He shouldn't be tried with the others. Feather and Scar were horrible. Evil. But Talon was . . ." I have no words to describe what he was. "He tried to help me, and he let me go, when the others were away. I would have escaped if I hadn't run into Scar on the way to find help. All of that should be taken into account. He should get a lesser sentence or whatever."

"He is still a kidnapper."

"But he did it for his brother! And his dad. You said yourself they deserve justice. Maybe that could start by not sentencing Talon in the same way as the others."

"It is impossible for me to think about what you have suffered these last couple of weeks. I am grateful that someone treated you with respect and kindness, but it is only what you deserved. These people stole you from your family in the most violent way possible, and then they kept you locked up. You must not equate a simple gesture in an extreme situation with . . . with anything more real. In a terrifying situation, even the most basic of humane treatment can feel like something special."

The sky is the metallic gray of predawn, a red glow illuminating the horizon. In the mess of bushes around me are the furtive rustles of tiny paws and snouts, while in the branches above, a bird trills in the new day. It is joined by the birds in nearby trees, until the whole wood is singing. The light in Talon's green eyes. My trembling fingers clasping his. The warmth of his body so close to me.

What I feel for Talon is special. It is not some syndrome, no matter what anyone says. But there is no point arguing with my dad.

A thought occurs to me. "How will you carry on as prime minister after all of this?"

"I won't. I tendered my resignation yesterday morning."

And he's only just telling me. Of course he is. Same old Dad choosing what truth he shares and when.

"You'll be heading back to Downing Street this afternoon," he explains. "I won't be coming with you, at least not today. The police want to take me in for questioning." We are walking slowly back to the main building. "They agreed to give me a chance to talk to you first."

"What made you tell the truth now? You could have kept hiding it. Lying to me. To everyone."

"After everything you've been through, I think you deserve the truth, don't you?"

Or is it that he suspected I would already know the truth by the time I was released?

When we reach the entrance to the building, Dad pauses before going inside. "I will most likely face charges for my part in this. I may even go to prison. My life—our lives—will change dramatically. There will be a lot of press attention, even more than before, if that's possible. And none of it will be pleasant."

A nurse wants to come through the doors, and Dad moves to let her pass. She eyes us both curiously, turning back to look at us again as she hurries down the path. I watch her go, wondering what she's thinking. "Does the public know yet?"

"There'll be a press conference later today. The deputy PM will lead it. There have been murmurings among journalists, of course, but so far they've been preoccupied with the story of your safe return."

"Will you go to the conference?"

"I'll give a statement. The party feels it might be better if I keep a low profile for a while."

"No one wants to be seen with you."

"No. I will have to face the journalists eventually, but I will put that off a little longer if I can."

"What will you do, now you're not PM?" I ask.

"I honestly don't know, Bobs," he says. "I just don't know." With his head bowed, I can see a bald patch on the top of his head that I swear wasn't there at Christmas. I wonder when my dad got so old, and when did I start to notice? Before, my parents were just that, parents. They told me when to go to bed and what to eat and what time to be home and to do my schoolwork. The world has shifted. I'll never take what Dad says at face value again just because he says it. From now on, I'm going to ask questions and make my own decisions about things.

"We should go inside," he says. "They'll be waiting to take you home. Your mother is dying to see you. I shouldn't hold you up any longer."

"Politics isn't everything."

"Isn't it?"

"No. And, hey, maybe now you'll spend some actual time with your family, for real, rather than just for the cameras."

"That was always real. I'm aware I haven't always been the greatest of fathers and that living in Downing Street has not been easy on you all. I have made some bad choices. This is by far the worst of all. So many people suffered for it. . . ."

"So what are you going to do?"

"I'm going to spend every waking minute for the rest of my life putting it right. And I'm going to apologize, loudly and to everyone." He half smiles. "There's a first time for everything, after all."

I hesitate, one hand on the glass door that leads inside. "I reckon we're going to be all right, you know."

"I hope so." His eyes have teared up again. "I really hope so. Go on now. The car is waiting to take you home." Then he smiles. "I know that look. You've got something more to ask me."

There's only one other thing that matters now. "Where's Talon?"

CHAPTER EIGHTEEN

Dad and I are flying to Paris in an hour. Mum comes into my room just as I am packing my new denim skirt, the one Mum says is too short, but I think goes great with thick tights and my gray biker boots. I scrunch it up and ram it deep into the folds of my duffel bag. I needn't have bothered, though. She isn't looking at me. She sits down on my bed, running her fingers over my eiderdown, a smile tattooed on her face. "I want you to have fun in Paris. Don't get caught up in your father's mad schemes, and don't get stuck in the hotel while he works. Get out and see the city. Who knows when you'll get another chance. Be your own person. Don't . . . don't become a clone of your dad. Promise me. Promise me you'll make your own choices, and not the ones he wants you to make. If—when— the time comes, remember what I've said. Don't be him, Robyn. I want something better for you."

Millbank is packed with tourists. The police motorcyclists have to flash their sirens to clear space. Neither of the two special-ops officers in the car has said a word since we left the hospital. As we turn onto Whitehall, I shift uncomfortably in the seat. My body finally realizes what it's gone through. Everything is hurting, like I've been through a spin cycle and my skin has shrunk. It's hurting my insides to have blood pumping through my veins.

The paparazzi are out in force today, packed hungrily around the Downing Street gates. I wonder if the press conference has just finished. Armed police officers try to force them back onto the pavement. "Be through in a minute," one of the officers in the car says. I don't answer. I stare straight ahead. The paps will be pressing their cameras up against the dark glass, hoping to catch a glimpse of the daughter of the disgraced PM. I won't show any emotion.

The car slows, and the journalists swarm over us like insects. They slam their fists on the car roof and shove their cameras up against the windows. My fingers whiten with the tension in my hands. *Do not cry, Robyn. Do not cry.* I retreat into my head, conjuring up the silence of that wood behind the farmhouse in my mind. The sound of the birds' cheerful chirps and Talon's whistling. The mud soft under my fingers.

One of the journalists hits my window, making me jump. "Give us a smile, Robyn," someone shouts. Another yells, "Glad to be home?" A third voice, louder and clearer than the rest, adds, "How do you feel about the shocking revelations about your dad and Bell-Barkov?"

My fingers clutch one another tightly, and I have to suck in the breath through my nose.

"Steady, miss," the officer beside me says. "Almost there now."

It feels like we will be swallowed up by the plague of journalists. The light inside the car darkens to night as bodies press up tighter and tighter against it.

At last we are through the gate and it is closing behind us, shutting the press pack on one side and us on the other. My breath unhitches. My lungs expand. We draw up to the curb of Number 10. Externally it is exactly the same as it has been for the last two hundred and something years. How many thousands of secrets have been hidden behind these thick brick walls? How many decisions have been made here for "the good of the nation"?

An officer follows me across the famous black-and-white-checkered hallway of Number 10. The place is even more chaotic than usual. Aides and secretaries fly about, gathering together files and the other paraphernalia of my dad's occupancy. Somewhere in the background the shredder is working overtime, probably destroying any other little secrets that my dad doesn't want anyone to find out about.

Just as we reach the stairs, a woman comes through the adjoining door to Number 11, smacking right into me. The papers she is carrying flutter to the floor. She swears.

Recognition fills her eyes as she looks at me. She opens her mouth. It hangs like that for a couple of seconds while her eyes become little round Os.

The officer clamps a reassuring hand on my shoulder. "Upstairs we go, miss," he says. "Your mother is waiting for you." The woman finally remembers her manners and closes her mouth. I sense her eyes on me as I begin to climb the stairs. I will not miss this place. I will not miss constantly being watched, monitored, and gossiped about.

Mum is sitting on the top step of the first landing. Something about her posture makes me think she's been there a long time. On seeing me, she stands. Then it's like there's something wrong with her legs, or she's just forgotten how to use them, because she's falling. I run full tilt to catch her. And as my arms go around her, I accept that it's over.

I'm free.

We hold each other for a long time.

I'll never again say that I'm too old to be hugged. I don't even mind when she starts crying because of my hair.

"It'll grow back," I say. "You hated my fringe anyway." We pull apart from each other, and she sees the bandage on my hand. "It's nothing. Honest."

"None of this is nothing," she says, a steely tone in her voice I've never heard before. "But you're home now. That's all that matters. Dear God, when that man took you . . . You have no idea. I wanted to be with you the second they found you, but they wouldn't let me. Protocol or some such rubbish. I will not miss all that, I must say. I can't wait to get back to Kensington and get everything sorted. Oh, my darling, I wish we could have taken you straight there and saved you all of this."

"I wanted to come back To say good-bye."

"Your father told you about Michael and Bell-Barkov and that little boy? I just can't believe it. It's too awful."

"Well," I say, "at least we don't have to live here anymore."

"No. No more Goldfish Bowl for us."

This place has been our prison and our protection for four years. I have hated the high walls and the barbed gates and the constant surveillance, and yet I have hidden behind them. Soon they'll be gone, and we'll have nothing then to shield us from the questions and the camera bulbs.

"It's not over, is it?"

"No, Robyn, I think it's only just beginning."

Poppy is lying on her bed, legs up against the wall, so that she doesn't get varicose veins. She turns her head as I enter her room, and we stare at each other, my best friend and me. So much has happened to me in the last thirteen days that I wonder how I will ever squeeze back into my old life. Then Poppy smiles. "Hello," she says, her voice thick.

"I can't believe you're leaving. You're just back and you're leaving again."

"No space in Downing Street for a corrupt PM. The British public are funny like that." It's a stupid thing to say, and Poppy doesn't laugh. Instead she opens a drawer in her bedside table.

"They retrieved this from the car. Your mum gave it to me to look after."

I take my beloved SLR from her. "Did she? Why?"

"I don't think she wanted to look at it anymore, in case . . ."

In case I didn't come back.

She is pressed up against the bed, her arms wrapped around herself. "You missed a great party at Millie's. Can't believe you made me go alone."

I flick the camera on, and Poppy's face smiles up at me. It's the photo I took on the day I was taken.

"And again my nose looks massive," Poppy says, coming to stand behind me so she can stare at the camera screen.

"I told you—the camera never lies."

Poppy rests her head on my shoulder, but not before I see her eyes bright with unshed tears. I can't cry. Not yet. I put my arms around her. Her tears drop onto my shoulder, salt mingling with the jasmine scent of Poppy's hair.

Behind me, there is a squeak, and then I feel Addy barrel into my legs. I lift her up, clutching her between us while Mum hovers in the doorway, pretending that she isn't crying.

And with my best friend's arms about me and my little sister's legs wrapped around me, I know that it is going to be all right. There are some things that never change no matter how far you go. There are some things you can always find your way back to.

CHAPTER NINETEEN

There are three guards in the corridor outside his room. Each one looks at me long and hard as Gordon explains who I am and why I am here. As the third one steps out of my way, Gordon presses a hand lightly on my back. "Ten minutes."

How can I say good-bye in ten minutes?

I push open the door and go in. The room is painted a dirty cream, with faded striped curtains. It is ridiculously early, a little after seven in the morning. We are hoping to avoid the press. He's reading a book, but he puts it down as soon as he sees me. "You came."

At the sound of his voice, a thousand memories fill my head. So much has happened between us. How can we ever fit all the pieces together?

"Yeah." My hand is still on the door handle.

"Are you leaving again already?"

"I shouldn't have come."

"I'm glad you did."

My hand is slick with sweat.

"How are your mum and sister?" he asks.

"Coping." Barely. Moving out of Downing Street has been a nightmare—the constant press intrusion, the endless police questions, the packing, the unpacking. And Mum is like a zombie. She hated being the PM's wife, but she hates being the wife of a disgraced ex-PM even more. Dad has been with the police a lot, "helping with their inquiries."

Talon thumbs the pages of his book, looking uncomfortable. This is my last chance to see him. I don't want to waste it.

"When are they moving you?" I ask, crossing the room to sit down on the chair by his bed. Talon has been refused bail. He is considered a flight risk. As soon as the doctors are happy that he has no brain injuries from the knock to the head the police gave him, he will be taken straight to prison to await trial.

"Tomorrow. How did you get permission to come here?"

"Gordon brought me."

"Gordon?"

"My dad's bodyguard. He called in a favor with his old friends in the police to get me in here. I should go soon."

"So you keep saying. I didn't ask you to visit me."

My skin burns crimson. Why did I assume he'd want to see me? What is left to say? Even though I'm free, he will always be my kidnapper.

I stand up and move over to the window. It is chilly for April, and a misty haze fogs up the glass. I wipe it away. There's a morning frost, a delicate lace arching over the leaves and bushes outside. The ice makes the trees, even the road running between them, look fragile, vulnerable, as though one harsh breath could blow it all away.

I press my palm flat against the glass, leaving my handprint, remembering too late that I am not supposed to have been here. This is my only chance to talk to him. I will remember this conversation for the rest of my life. Why am I wasting it? I don't want to regret anything. I turn to face him. "Do you remember when you said you wished we'd met under different circumstances?"

He nods.

"We never would have met, and that means I can't regret everything that's happened to me."

"Then neither do I."

"Even if it means going to prison?"

"I deserve to go to prison, Robyn."

"But it's not fair."

He smiles at the petulant tone in my voice and holds out his hand. I take it, closing the distance between us in less than a heartbeat. His fingers lace with mine, drawing me closer still.

The clock on the wall says 7:05. Five minutes left. The bruises on his arms and neck are pulpy and black like rotten avocado. Movement is painful for him.

"You might not have to go to prison, you know," I say.

"I spoke to Gordon. He said that if you were willing to testify against Scar and Feather, your punishment would be reduced. They would take into account your age, and they may be more lenient."

It is a long time before Talon responds. My hand looks tiny, like a small bird, in his. "They'd never keep their word. They'd still send me to prison."

"But they might not! You could get a suspended sentence."

He shakes his head. "It wouldn't be right. No one forced me into it. I'm not a kid. I'm nineteen. I knew what I was doing and I did it anyway. I kidnapped you. I bought the chloroform. I helped pack the ropes. No one forced me to do any of that. I deserve to be punished."

The fledgling sunlight streams through the window. "Dad says a small humane act in a terrifying situation can mean more than it should."

"Robyn, I am going to prison. You have to forget about me."

"I can't."

"Then you're an idiot." But he is smiling. "I can't do it. I can't give up Feather for my own gain. And what good would it do? You and me, we couldn't . . ."

I sigh, my body expelling the used air and my faded hope at the same time. "I know, but let's pretend that we can. Just for a little while." There's something I have to say, and I'm afraid if I don't do it now, I won't be brave enough. "I never questioned him, my dad, not properly. About anything. I didn't think enough about what him being prime minister meant and the sorts of decisions he would be making. Mum tried to warn me, but I didn't listen."

"You're only sixteen—"

"That's no excuse. I was suspicious in Paris. Something was wrong, but I didn't want to know, so I didn't ask."

"You're asking now. Do you remember what I said in the wood?"

It takes a whole lifetime of decisions to make you who you are.

I nod.

"I think on the whole you haven't done too badly. In fact, I'd say you were pretty damn special."

"Thank you," I say quietly.

"Will your dad face trial?"

"They don't know yet. It could be months before they gather the evidence."

"What will you do, you and your mum and sister?"

"Live in Kensington. Try to avoid the press. I'll go back to school. I should hate my dad for what he's done. But I don't, and I don't want him to go to prison. It's so unfair. He's no longer prime minister and yet we still don't get him back. I'm sorry. I sound pathetic saying that after everything you've lost."

"One loss doesn't trump another. Anyway, it's working

out. I've been in touch with my mum. She is getting better, slowly. And there's going to be a full investigation. We'll finally get justice for my brother."

But Talon won't be there to see it. He draws my straggly, ratty hair through his hands. "You know it kind of suits you like this."

"Hostage chic?"

"Well, maybe you should get a professional to cut it. But I like it shorter. You can see more of your face."

I put my hand on my hair. "I want to grow it a bit, but yeah, I agree. I don't think I'll grow it long again. Maybe to my chin or something."

I sit back then to take in his eyes, the freckles on his nose, the curve of his cheekbones. I will never see him again. His hand tightens around mine. *Don't think about the future,* he seems to say. So I don't. I bend in and kiss him tenderly and slowly, as if we have the rest of our lives together instead of barely four minutes. He draws me closer to him, kissing me harder and longer. I slide down on the bed, resting on my elbow, so he doesn't have to twist his neck to kiss me. He flinches as I accidentally knock his ribs.

"It's just a twinge. It's nothing." He grins. "Don't stop. This is . . . nice."

"Nice? Is that the best word you can think of?"

"I've had better."

"Oh, really?" I flick him in the ribs. I barely touch him, but he cries out. "Talon. God, I'm sorry."

He tugs down a few jerky breaths. "It's okay. It's okay . . . just . . . give me a second."

Scar beat him up. And he was hit over the head by a police officer. There's also going to be an investigation into the special forces' handling of the hand-over. Dad said he didn't know anything about them deciding to use a fake Marble. Do I believe him? I'm not sure. Anyway, the man who shot Feather could face prosecution.

"Feather is still here somewhere too. Some infection from that gunshot wound." I hope her arm falls off.

"I know."

"You've seen her?" I ask.

He shakes his head. "One of the nurses . . . I asked her to find out what was happening."

"Oh, right."

"It was her who shot your dad. I thought maybe she was bluffing in the cell. I can't believe she let Marble take the blame. She had this messed-up idea that she'd be a hero when she got your father to release him in exchange for you." He looks like he can't believe it, even though he knows it's true. After a moment or two, he says, "Lean against me again. It was . . ." He pauses and grins. "Nice."

"Apart from the searing pain in your ribs."

"Yeah, apart from that."

I lie back down again, careful not to go anywhere near his rib cage this time. "I'll keep visiting you, if you like, while you're here. I can come again tomorrow morning, before they . . . before they . . ."

"I won't be here tomorrow." A tear slides down his cheek. I brush it away with my thumb, but another follows it and another and another. There are too many for me to catch.

"I'll come every day, even when you're in . . ." *Prison.* "I will. I will." And I whisper it over and over, as though that will somehow make it come true, as though my words will sweep away all the obstacles between us.

He drops his head on my chest. His tears are flowing freely now, his body jerking as he cries silently against me. He is murmuring something, and I lean in closer to hear it. "Forget me," he whispers. "Forget me."

The wood is dark. The special ops are chasing us, but in here, in this cave of leaves and branches, it is quiet and still. Talon's eyes drop to my lips, to my eyes, and back again. My hands are shaking as they slide around him and up his back. I love you. I love you. I love you. . . .

In my dreams I am forever in that wood, my fingers scrunching in the dirt as I listen to the goldcrests and the sparrows and the robins chatter in the tree above. Sometimes Talon is with me, lying stretched out on the grass and laughing or else making his funny animal calls. Sometimes—and those are the best dreams—I am in his arms. We are so close that we are breathing into each other, our lips millimeters apart.

Most often, though, I am in that wood alone. When I reach for Talon, his patch of crumpled grass will be warm, as if he has only just left me.

Nine months later

CHAPTER TWENTY

Granny and Grandpa's house looms ahead of me, a squat gray slab that has been in Mum's family since her great-great-great-great-grandfather (give or take a few greats) built it on a strip of land gifted to him by the king in fifteen hundred and something. It's the second of January and freezing. Six inches of snow fell over Christmas. It's beautiful, but even I am getting bored of it now. There are only so many photos of white-covered stuff that you can take before snow blindness sets in. Plus, the heating broke in Granny and Grandpa's house yesterday, so it's even colder here than usual. But the estate in Cheshire is the only place where we can be quiet and alone, without the constant flashing of camera bulbs and the never-ending questions. I sometimes feel like I had more freedom when I was a hostage.

We fled here the week before Christmas, and no one's mentioned going back to Kensington yet. We'll have to soon, though. School term starts next week, and I'm pretty much screwed. No one's admitted it yet, but we all know I'm going to have to repeat the year. In some ways I don't mind. I mean, I wouldn't want to actually repeat the year, event by event, but maybe by redoing Year 12, I can somehow eradicate the last twelve months.

I can't believe it was exactly a year ago that we were in Paris. I've had a very different sort of start to the year. Grandpa is still really pissed at Dad, but Granny is mostly just "disappointed," which is worse somehow. Grandpa blusters and curses; Granny is silent and withdrawn, and she has suddenly started looking every minute of her seventy-two years.

After cutting across the front lawn, I trudge around to the side entrance to the house. My camera case bumps against my hip. I haven't taken any pictures this morning. There wasn't anything to capture, just endless whiteness. I didn't even hear any birds. Yesterday I spotted a couple of robins making a nest down by the lake.

I fling my boots off in the pantry, stopping when I'm halfway across the flagstones to go back and line them up properly. I don't want to add to Granny's stress and anxiety—mess of any kind makes her crazy. It's lucky I did, because she's in the kitchen, stirring porridge on the stove.

"Nice walk?" she asks.

"Cold walk." I line my mittens up on the radiator to dry. "You look tired. Can't Marion do that?"

"Marion always burns it. And I can just about manage to make my own porridge. Not in the grave yet."

I kiss her leathery cheek. "Is Dad up?"

"Blue Room. With your mother. Writing his letters." Granny sounds like she is sucking on a mouthful of lemons.

"It's a good thing, Granny."

"A good thing would have been him not getting us into this mess in the first place. But there, I'm an old woman. No one takes any notice of me."

I grin at her and go out into the hallway to peek through the open door to the Blue Room, which is the long, narrow living room at the front of the house. Dad is sitting in the large armchair by the window, his head back, his eyes closed, and a blanket over his knees. He looks like an old man. His shoulder hurts more in the cold, and over the last few months, he seems to have increasingly lost the use of his arm. He is in near-constant pain now. The doctors can't explain it. They've suggested that it might be a damaged nerve and have advised all sorts of treatments. Dad resists most of them. "It's my past sins catching up with me," he says. "If you go up into Grandpa's attic, you'll find a ravaged painting of me. All the evil I've done in my life visible on that portrait."

To which Mum always laughs and says, not unkindly, "The evil you've done isn't hidden in the attic. It's reported in the press on a daily basis."

"There's another letter from the chief medical officer at Bradford General," Mum says now. She's perched on the chair beside my dad. "All his patients who received Amabim-F had bad side effects. Shortness of breath and a rash."

Dad met Talon's mum a few months back to apologize personally for delaying the truth coming out. Now he and Mum are looking to set up a charity that supports all kidney-disease sufferers and their families. I want them to call it the Jeremy Fletcher Foundation. I wrote to Talon in prison to ask him what he thought, but he never replied. I've written him a letter every week since I last saw him. He hasn't replied to any of them.

Dad leans forward to take the letter from Mum's hand, wincing in pain as he does so. Mum presses her hand to his forehead. "Do you need more pills?" she asks softly.

Dad shakes his head, and Mum kisses him lightly on the cheek.

I creep quietly away before either of them sees me. Unbelievably, Mum and Dad are closer than I've ever seen them. I'm pleased that something positive has come out of all this, but it hurts, too. There's a distance between me and Dad these days, and I don't know how to close it. In fact, there's a distance between me and everyone now. Even me and Poppy. She tries to understand, but she can't. No one can. No one knows what I went through. No one except Talon, and he won't reply to any of my letters.

Talon, Feather, and Scar are in prison. Feather and Scar got the longest sentences—fifteen years. Eight for kidnapping and seven for attempted murder. In a bizarre twist, it turns out that my father wasn't the target in Paris. Feather had been aiming for Michael. Michael's room had been near our suite in the hotel, and Dad had had Michael's coat over his head when we ran for the car. It seems that Dad has his friend's ridiculous taste in clothing to thank for his shoulder injury.

The shooting, or rather the media storm that came after it, was what led to my kidnapping. During her trial, Feather revealed that after seeing the scale of the coverage on the shooting in Paris, she knew that when it came to getting her brother released, she had to switch focus from Michael to my dad. But she didn't want to kidnap him—it was too problematic, not least from a logistical point of view. I was less well-protected and arguably a better victim anyway. I was an "innocent" *and* the PM's daughter. The press would go crazy for the story, not only in the UK but around the world. Plus, my father actually had the power to release Marble, or at least influence the decision.

The judge was lenient with Talon after all. Perhaps something I said registered with someone. He's serving four years. They reckon he could be out in two for good behavior. Two years still seems like a very long time.

Marble has been released. All charges dropped.

The trials of Michael Bell and Bell-Barkov are due to start in the new year. Michael's facing charges of gross negligence and manslaughter. Bell-Barkov will probably be fined, along with Glindeson, the company that oversaw the drug's trial. Amabim-F has been taken off the market.

I'm heading up the stairs to find Addy when my mobile rings. I left it on the table in the hall. I tuck my hair behind my ear—it's chin-length now—before answering it. "Hello."

A voice I could never forget says, "Hello, Robyn."

I slide down on to the floor. "Hi."

"Hello."

"Hi," I say again.

"You said that already." It's funny how you can hear someone smile. "There's a robin that sits on the fence when I'm doing outside exercise. It makes me think of you."

My knuckles are white from gripping the handset.

"Robyn? Are you still there?"

I make a noise that is somewhere between a cry and the word "yes."

"I got your letters."

Come on, Robyn. Formulate an actual sentence. "You . . . you didn't reply."

"No."

"But you're calling me now."

"Yes."

I remember the last time I saw him, how I held him as he cried and whispered, *Forget me. Forget me.*

"I can't."

"Can't what?" he asks.

"Forget you."

There's a thumping in my rib cage like something's trying to escape.

"Me neither," Talon says.

"So what do we do?"

"I don't know."

"I could . . . I mean . . . if you wanted me to . . ."

"We don't have a future, you know that. I mean, how could we?"

"I know," I say, thinking of his hands in my hair.

"You should really just move on, even if I can't."

"I know." His breath on my neck.

"Find someone else."

"Definitely." His mouth on my lips.

"So . . . you'll come and see me?"

Dad says that words are a powerful weapon. A single one can change a destiny. Imagine what two could do.

"You bet."